Hitchhiker

Hitchhiker

Copyright 2024 © Nettie G. Leeflang
Cover photo credit:
Sebastian Palomino; Chermiti Mohamed on Pexels.com
ISBN 978-1-0689861-0-9
www.nettieleeflang.com
All rights reserved.
No part of this publication may be reproduced in any form, or by any means, electronic or mechanical, including photocopying, recording, or any information browsing, storage, or retrieval system, without permission in writing from the author.
First printed in Dutch by:
© Uitgeverij De Banier, Apeldoorn 2019
Omslagontwerp en vormgeving: Albert Bloemert
ISBN 978 94 0290 7254
c-NUR 340-060
www.debanier.nl

Hitchhiker

Nettie Leeflang

www.nettieleeflang.com

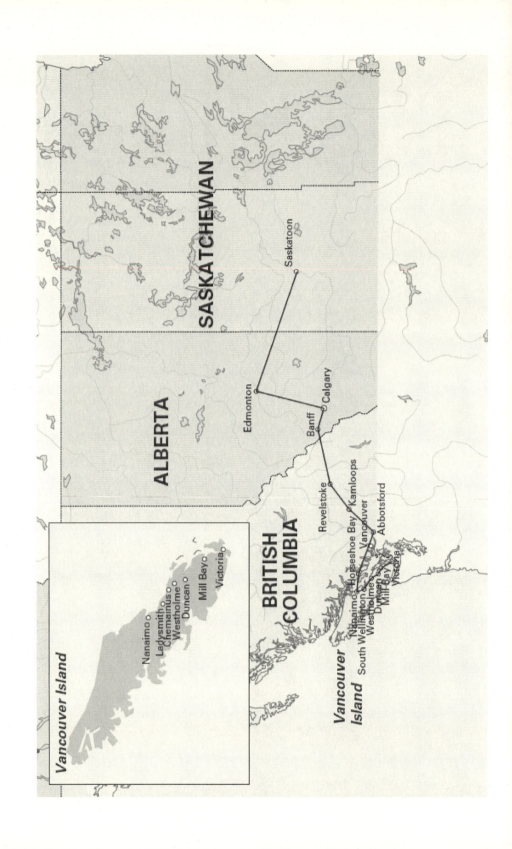

Psalm 136:1

Oh, give thanks to the Lord, for He is good!
For His mercy endures forever.

**

A big thank-you to my friends Caroline and Barb for helping me translate those funny Dutch idioms into common-sense English.

Table of contents

Foreword 9
1. Father and Mother 16
2. Grandpa and Grandma 19
3. No roses without thorns 26
4. Graduation party 30
5. That black thing 35
6. Preparations 37
7. The train trip 41
8. Visiting the pastor 46
9. Beautiful Banff 54
10. Tortilla 61
11. Oh, Boy 64
12. Warning 68
13. First Nations stories 75
14. On the ferry 80
15. South Wellington 87
16. Destination or starting point? 93
17. Warrior or Worrier? 97
18. Labour Day weekend 101
19. Cindy 109

20. Job hunting	115
21. McDonald's	122
22. Poor Amy	125
23. Banker Jayden	131
24. Thanksgiving	139
25. Halloween	144
26. A place to settle	147
27. Haunting lies	151
28. Shivering cold	156
29. Renewed hope	159
30. Website	162
31. Caught	166
32. He's got the whole world in His hands	174
33. Christmas parade	179
34. Everyone knows better	183
35. Turmoil in the camp	189
36. New Year's Eve	194
37. The old man	205
38. City Council meetings	208
39. Newspaper	212
40. The End	215
Epilogue	219

Foreword

That next week, the new school year was about to begin. I drove, together with my oldest son, the 45-minute drive to the ferry in Nanaimo. He was a student at the British Columbia Institute of Technology in Vancouver on the mainland. It seemed he was heading toward a successful future. With his clear outlook on life, I didn't have to worry about him.

The drizzling rain made the asphalt shine. I turned on my windshield wipers. The truck in front of me sprayed my window with dirty water from its rear tires.

Ten kilometres before Nanaimo, a girl with her thumb out, was hitchhiking on the other side of the highway, heading in the opposite direction. She seemed almost overpowered by her wet backpack, which rose high above her head. Beside her walked a dog of an uncertain breed. His head was drooping as if he, too, was carrying a heavy load.

"I'll pick you up on my way back if nobody else has picked you up yet," I told the girl telepathically.

Fifteen minutes later, we reached Nanaimo. We had left the rain behind us; here the sun was shining. It was quiet in the city. The businesses along the highway weren't open yet. A group of people stood talking in front of the Salvation Army, but there were no other people in sight. It seemed like a perfect September morning.

I said goodbye to my son in the parking lot at the ferry terminal. The place was buzzing with the parents of students coming and going, bringing their studying children to the ferry. The atmosphere was filled with the expectations of promising futures.

On my way home, I had already forgotten about the girl with the backpack, but just past the gas station in South Wellington, a little before the airport, I saw her again. Her dog lingered alongside her. Someone had probably dropped her off at the gas station, and she had started walking again, hoping for someone else to take her further. She carried a white, square sign with the word 'Victoria' on it. Unfortunately, she was walking where the emergency lane was only half the width of my car, so I had nowhere to pull over. I let the two cars behind me pass.

I parked my car alongside the highway. I stepped out, opened the trunk, and beckoned her to come. She tried to run. The heavy backpack jolted precariously on her back. Her dog also had a hard time hurrying forward. I helped her put her backpack in the trunk. To my surprise, the backpack was not very heavy. This showed me she was either weakened or just too small for such a load.

"Your dog can go in the back too," I said.

She stooped down and lifted him in the back seat of the car.

"I can bring you to Westholme. That's where I'm going off the highway. In Westholme there's a farmers market where a lot of people shop. From there, you can try to hitchhike with somebody else."

She looked at me from under her grey toque, which was glued to her head. Spiky, wet stands of red hair peeked out from under the hat. The look in her bright blue eyes made me think of someone on the run.

I closed the trunk, and we got into the car. She sat in the passenger seat beside me.

"What's your name?" I asked.

"Nadia," she said.

"You want to go to Victoria?"

She nodded and looked at me as if she expected me to make a critical comment.

"Nice," I said. "Victoria is a beautiful city. Many historical buildings, stunning ocean."

"Yup," she said.

Interested, I asked, "What are you going to do there?"

She shrugged. "I don't know yet."

"How long are you planning to stay?"

"Till the winter is gone, and I'll take it from there."

An alarm bell went off in my head, and all of a sudden, I noticed the musty smell she had brought into the car. I suspected that it wasn't just from the rain.

"Where do you come from?" I asked.

"Saskatchewan," she answered.

I was surprised she was still answering my questions.

"So, actually, from what I understand," I asked carefully, " you don't really have a plan?"

"No," she said.

Meanwhile, we had driven past Nanaimo Airport and were approaching Ladysmith.

"Do you have relatives?" I dared to ask.

"Yes, but I don't want to see them ever again," she burst out.

I glanced at her sideways, and her eyes, which until then had seemed insecure and on guard, were now spewing fire. I realized that if I were to say something wrong, she would force me to stop the car and get out.

Shrugging, I said as casually as possible, "Relatives can sometimes be the biggest pain in the neck you can imagine."

While I paid attention to the road, I felt the tension she had built up fading away.

"It seems like you have experience," she said.

"For sure," I answered and left it at that. I didn't intend to tell my story; I wanted to hear hers.

"Apparently, you do too," I smiled encouragingly at her.

"Yes," she said. She kept quiet for a couple of minutes. We had left Ladysmith behind us and Chemainus came into sight. It wouldn't be long before we entered Westholme, and our conversation would come to an end. I still didn't know much about her.

"Well," I gambled, "you're old enough to build your own life. You don't need relatives for that."

"Yep," she said again, "last week was my 19th birthday. They can't control me anymore."

"But you need a goal," I pressed. "You can't just live in Victoria and hope you'll have a good life without knowing what direction you're going in."

"That's what I've got to figure out," she admitted.

"Is there something you would like to do? Do you have a hobby or something that makes you very happy while you're doing it?"

She didn't have to think long before responding. "I write," she said passionately, "but I don't know if I'll pursue that."

We exited the highway. I parked at the Farmer's Market and we got out of the car.

"Do you need anything?" I asked and pointed at the store.

"No, thank you," she said. "At the moment I've everything I need."

I helped her pull her backpack from the trunk and lift it onto her back again.

"Thank you very much for the ride," she said and shook my hand.

"You're very welcome," I said. I searched the pocket of my coat and found my business card. I gave it to her. "I want you to call me when you're in trouble and can't fix it by yourself.

But mostly, I want you to call me to let me know you're okay."

She took the card and promised to call me.

"Come on, Boy," she said to her dog. "Let's go."

She turned around, swaying, and waved. She walked back to the highway to wait for another ride. I drove home, hoping everything would turn out alright for her.

***

Today, it has been a year since she promised to call me. I had hoped she would keep her promise, but as the months went by, that hope faded. This morning, my phone rang. I picked it up, and a voice said, "It's me, Nadia."

My head started to spin. A thousand questions tumbled over each other. I wanted to ask them all, but she didn't give me a chance.

"Can you please come to Victoria?" she asked. "I would like to give you something."

I got into my car and drove from Westholme, as fast as the speed limit allowed, over the Malahat mountain to Victoria. An hour later, I met her at a colourful Mexican restaurant at Fisherman's Wharf. Again, it was the long weekend before Labour Day, and the wharf was bustling with tourists.

I bought us each a coffee and a chicken with coleslaw wrap. We sat down with our legs dangling over the edge of the wharf. The sound of the sloshing water against the dock gave me a summery, carefree feeling. Seagulls floated on the water in front of us, hoping for a piece of food. Now and then, the head of a seal popped out of the water. The sun reflected off the little waves.

I put on my sunglasses. Nadia wore a green toque, and her red hair sneaked out in curls from under it. Her vivid blue eyes were bright, and she looked at me, relaxed. Was this the nervous, directionless girl I had picked up from the highway a year ago? She had become a beautiful young woman with a confident personality.

Boy, her dog, quietly walked behind us and lay down beside Nadia on the dock. Occasionally, he turned his eyes towards me and then looked away again. From time to time, he sighed, as if life had been too hard for him.

I gathered some courage and asked the question that had occupied my thoughts for so long.

"How did you do this past year?"

Nadia smiled, grabbed her bag from the ground, and started rummaging through it. She pulled out a pile of papers and put it in my lap. '*Hitchhiker*' was written on the first page, and underneath it said '*by Nadia*'. In quotation marks, after it, was scribbled: '*I've got to come up with a pseudonym for this*'.

I looked at her and a big smile appeared on my face. "You've written a story!" I called out.

She nodded. "You can read it if you want."

I flipped through the pile of papers and read a couple of sentences.

"Amazing," I said. "Thank you."

"Do you see that guitar player?" Nadia asked, nodding her head towards a spot behind me where I heard music. I turned around and saw a young woman standing and playing the guitar. I estimated her to be in her late twenties. Beside her on the ground sat a young man about the same age. In front of her was an open guitar case into which people were tossing money.

"That's Cindy," said Nadia, "and that's Jayden sitting beside her. I'm writing about them too, in my story."

"Shall we go and chat with them?" I suggested.

"No, no," Nadia said, upset, "they're not my friends."

"Oh, I see," I said, "would you like to sit somewhere else, somewhere you can't see them?"

"No," replied Nadia, now in a calm voice, "it's okay."

"Tell me about them and the other people in your story," I urged her.

"Okay," agreed Nadia. She was silent for a while as if she didn't know where to start.

"It was cold and wet," she finally said, "so different from today with the sun shining, making everything look so happy. Everything around us was filthy and gloomy. We often had no hope it would ever be better."

I glanced over the bay and let my eyes rest on the mountains on the other side. They were hazy from the warmth of the sun shining on them. I let Nadia talk. Sometimes I asked a question, and on she went, dragging me through the dreary parks and streets of Victoria in wintertime.

Two hours later, I drove back to Westholme and didn't turn on the radio once. Nadia's story echoed in my ears, and I could hardly wait to read her manuscript. It wasn't until after dinner that I got a chance to start reading. I nestled myself in my lazy chair with a mug of coffee and turned the first page.

1. Father and Mother

The day I was born, my father decided to move in with his girlfriend, leaving my mother alone with their three children. My brother was four and my sister two years old when I arrived to complete our family. Years later, my father told me that my mother cried the entire week my grandma was there to support her postpartum. When my grandma went back to Ontario, where she and my grandpa lived, my mother stopped crying.

My mother's crying turned into bitterness. She did the housework and demanded that we help her. As soon as we were able, we did dishes, folded laundry, scrubbed toilet bowls, and, the instant we were big enough to stand on a ladder, we washed the windows too. We didn't dare say 'no' to our mother's orders, but we found ways to escape doing chores or would pin the job on another sibling.

We spent the weekends at my father's house, where he lived with his girlfriend. We wondered which was better: working for our mother during the week until all the chores were done and watching her drink, slumped on the couch in front of the TV, or staying at my father's over the weekends. There, we listened to him and his girlfriend yell at each other and watched how they made each other's lives miserable.

My father had a construction company and made good money. That's why my mother didn't have to work outside the home. She was able to live off the alimony my father sent her every month. Slowly, she transformed into a negative, lazy woman who didn't care about her appearance or health. She gained weight to sickening proportions, which led to even more work being dumped on our young shoulders.

I had the bad luck of being the youngest and smallest. In a normal, functioning family, that might have been an advantage, and they would have been considerate of my age. But nothing like that happened in our family. My mother favoured my brother and sister, who felt it was their right to humiliate me and use me as a servant. I think my mother blamed me for driving my father away, although she never said it out loud.

My days were filled with going to school, doing chores, and, if there was time left, doing homework. It wasn't surprising my grades were low. Because of that, I was ridiculed at home, and even more chores were piled on me. After all, I wasn't able to study, so why bother giving me time to do my homework?

At school, I was a loner. I was afraid that if I made a friend, she would want to come with me to my house. I tried to prevent that. I was ashamed of my family, so I kept to myself as much as possible. Sometimes the kids would pull my red hair or laugh at my freckles. I just ignored them, but my stomach always cramped up.

My father met his girlfriend at a barbeque he had organized for his employees. Everybody brought a partner, and that's how he met Barbara, who was still married to John at the time. Of course, this didn't happen overnight, but eventually, she and my father started dating. It was when my mother was pregnant with me that my father must have hatched a plan to leave her. For reasons unknown to me, he chose to leave my mother the day I was born. Years later, the missing pieces of this puzzle were revealed to me, and I understood what had happened around the time of my birth.

John, Barbara's ex-husband, took the blow better than my mother. He sat with his hands in his hair for a little while, but he quickly turned over a new leaf and married Georgette, whom he had met in the pub. He couldn't stand my father anymore and changed employers. I never heard my father say he regretted losing a good employee. Maybe he thought it was convenient to not have to endure hostile looks and punches below the belt at work anymore.

The first week after I was born, my mother made a few whiny attempts to change my father's mind and get him to come back to her. During that same week, he paid a visit to see me. My grandma called him selfish and told my mother, in his presence, that he'd always been useless to his family. Either my mother agreed with her or she realized she wasn't strong enough to endure his indifferent stubbornness, but after that, she never asked him again to come back to her. In the years that followed, she took out her humiliation from being left for somebody else on my brother and sister, and particularly on me.

2. Grandpa and Grandma

The highlight of each year was when we took the train to see my grandpa and grandma in Toronto. We would board the train in Saskatoon, and three days later, we would arrive at the station in Toronto. Bij then, the book I had brought to read would be finished. The hide-and-seek games would degrade into whining and bullying. We would sleep poorly for two nights in a row, and I was always relieved to step onto the railway platform with my suitcase in hand.

My grandpa used to pick us up in his white, antique Buick Skylark convertible. At 16, he had bought it new in 1966, right after acquiring his driver's license. My mother would sit in the front seat beside Grandpa, and the three of us, my brother, my sister, and I were in the back seat. The ruffling of the wind in my hair and the setting sun on my face made me feel free. In Grandpa's slow pace, we cruised out of Toronto to the acreage my grandparents owned on the outskirts of town. Their house was built of brick and spacious enough to provide each of us with our own bedroom.

Typically, in the evening, the adults would drink their coffee on the porch. My bedroom was at the back of the house, so when my window was open, I could hear them talking. I would lie in bed, listening to their stories wafting in through the open window, but I could never hear enough to follow the conversation entirely. Although I would catch snippets of descriptions of people I didn't know or stories about Grandpa's work, I could never understand exactly what happened or what kind of work he did. Slowly, I would doze off to the murmur of their voices and the rustling of the leaves from the tall poplars around the house.

I felt safe at Grandpa and Grandma's house. I felt freed from the pressure always put on me to serve and slave for my family. I clearly remember the summer vacation before my 11th birthday in September. Grandma put my mother to work in the kitchen and ordered my brother and sister to pick all the apples from the apple tree. After they finished that, they had to pick the beans from the garden.
At first, they liked doing chores for Grandma, but very soon they started to complain.
"What's with Nadia not helping us?" they asked.
"She will have her turn soon," reassured Grandma.
Half an hour later, while my mother was peeling potatoes in the kitchen and my brother and sister were in the garden picking the beans, Grandma asked me to come with her to do some grocery shopping.
"That's our chore for today," she said and winked at me.
We drove in Grandma's red Smart car to the little village of Orangeville. We bought a couple of new socks for Grandpa and a box of chocolates for tea time. Grandma bought an ice cream for me.
"Come, young lady," she said, "we are going home."
She gave me her hand, and we walked past store windows, enjoying each other's company. A lady whom Grandma knew from church stopped to chat with us.
"Isn't that your granddaughter?" she asked. "What a big girl already, eh?"
Grandma wrapped her arm around my shoulder and pulled me close. "Yes, this is Nadia, my youngest granddaughter, my best friend."

I looked up at Grandma's happy face, and my eyes beamed. When I was with Grandma, it didn't feel awkward to be the centre of attention. I felt safe in her warm, genuine embrace. Nothing could ever break our friendship.
On the way back in the car, she asked me all kinds of things about home and school in Saskatoon.
"Do you have a nice teacher?" she asked.
I shrugged. "My teacher is nice," I said, "but he favours the students who are good."
"You're smart," said Grandma as if this was the most normal thing in the world.
I shrugged again, now shy because of the compliment.
"My marks are not great," I said softly.
"Oh, no?" she asked, surprised. "Why is that?"
I told her about all the chores I had to do which didn't leave me enough time to do my homework. She let me tell her everything and stayed quiet when I was done talking. She stopped the car for a red light, laid her hand on my knee, and said, "I'll see what I can do for you."
The traffic light turned green, and Grandma continued driving.
"Don't forget," she said, keeping her eyes on the road, "God sees and knows everything. You can go to Him for advice."
I nodded. "I know," I mumbled, but I didn't know how to hear His answer.

At home, Grandma walked into the kitchen and pulled my mother into the hallway by her sleeve. The door shut firmly behind them. I could hear Grandma talking, but I couldn't make out the words. However, I did hear what my mother said.
"That girl lies through her teeth," she shouted.

I fled the house and only came back inside when Grandpa came home from work. That evening, I had the privilege of sitting beside him at the dinner table, which made the angry looks from my mother less painful. I didn't want to think about the end of our visit or the trip back home.

My brother and sister had to help clear the table. They squirmed between the table and the counter, pushing and punching each other. My sister dropped a plate, which smashed into pieces with a loud clatter.

"Dummy," she yelled at my brother, "do you see what you did?"

Grandma handed me the compost bucket.

"Go feed the rabbit," she said softly, and then, in a stern voice to my sister, "Fetch the broom and the dustpan."

"It's his fault," my crying sister shouted. "He has to clean it up."

I ran out of the kitchen. At the back door, I put on my boots. I heard Grandpa shouting "Shut up," followed by screams from my brother and sister. I tiptoed back to the kitchen door to see what was happening. Grandpa stood between my brother and sister, pinching their ears between his thumbs and fingers. They struggled to free themselves from Grandpa's strong grip.

I sneaked back to the outside door and went to feed the rabbit. I petted his fur with one hand while he nibbled at the lettuce I offered him with the other. I began talking to him, marking the start of my storytelling. I didn't dare to write my stories down, but the rabbit wouldn't tell anyone. They were safe with him and would disappear in the stew at Christmas, too.

Years later, after I had saved up enough to buy my own computer, I finally felt confident enough to type out my stories, knowing my written ramblings were protected by a password that kept them safe from prying eyes.

My brother and sister didn't let the issue rest. They understood very well that I had the same workload at Grandpa and Grandma's, as they had in Saskatoon. It drove them crazy that I was favoured at my grandparent's home. To get even, they sought revenge by playing childish tricks on me, such as putting salt in my tea and hiding catchweed between my bedsheets. Their tricks weren't very creative, but I remained vigilant.

On the train back home, they managed to pull a dirty trick on me. During the day, we sat in our assigned seats, frequently walking back and forth to the washrooms and the dining car. During dinnertime, our seats were transformed into berths. My brother and sister slept on one side of the aisle, while my mother and I were on the other.

My mother didn't want to go to bed early and went to the bar car for a beer. She instructed us to stay in our berths but allowed us to read if we wanted. My brother and sister lay on their beds, each with a book in hand. Their curtains were slightly open, and occasionally one of them peeked through the gap to see if anything was happening in the aisle. Each time, they looked at me as well.

"Are you sleeping yet?" my brother asked.

I didn't respond. I'm sure he saw that I was awake. When my sister asked the same question five minutes later, I became suspicious. I grabbed my book and turned my face towards the window, my back to them. I read a few pages, but the rhythm of the train must have lulled me to sleep.

I woke up when my mother opened the aisle curtain. It was dark outside; we were passing through an area with no houses. I looked at the sky and saw the twinkling stars. Everything seemed peaceful.

At one point, we approached a small train station. The train slowed down and stopped. Our train car was too far from the platform to see who was boarding the train. As I leaned on my arm to get a better look, I felt something pulling at my hair. To my shock, my hair seemed stuck to the pillow. I tried to peel it loose, but it wouldn't budge.

"Mom," I screamed, "my hair got stuck."

"Don't be so stupid, girl," she replied, "you're dreaming."

"No, Mom, I'm not," I said, scared.

I heard snickering coming from the other side of the aisle and knew who had pranked me. My mother pulled at the pillow, and I screamed.

"Shut up, girl," she snapped.

She rummaged through her beauty case for scissors and she cut my hair loose from the pillow. Red chunks of hair still stuck to the pillow with blobs of glue in between. I touched my hair. Before, I had enough length to make a ponytail, but now strands fell beside my face.

I was furious. Incredibly furious. I clenched my teeth, and angry tears sprang to my eyes.

"Don't look so mad," my mother said, "you probably deserved it."

Infuriated, I turned my pillow to the clean side and laid my head down. One day, I promised myself, I would make them pay for this.

The next morning, the rising sun woke me up. I wanted to go to the glass-domed car upstairs to watch the passing scenery, but first, I had to convince myself that I wasn't afraid to go upstairs with my ridiculous hairstyle. My mother was still snoring, so I took her beauty case to the washroom. I started sweating bullets when I saw myself in the mirror above the sink. The uneven locks of hair sled through my fingers as panic crept up on me. Only two more weeks and I would have to return to school. That wasn't enough time to grow my hair back to its usual length.

With the help of bobby pins and an elastic, I made myself somewhat presentable. Timidly, I went upstairs to the glass-domed car, feeling insecure. It was already bustling with people, despite it being 6 a.m. Most of them were older. A friendly lady nodded at me, which gave me some encouragement. I wouldn't expect my brother and sister to be up so early; they usually preferred lounging around over waking up early. I wished I could pay them back, but I had no idea how.

That winter, in my last year of elementary school, Grandma died of a stroke. She was only 58 years old. This time, we didn't take the train but flew to Toronto. Everything beneath us was white with snow.

My mother, brother, and sister cried their eyes out at the funeral.

"What a soulless person you are," my mother sobbed when she saw I wasn't shedding any tears.

I didn't blame her. She couldn't see that my heart was crying from the pain I felt inside.

The next summer, we stayed with Grandpa, but it was never the same. Grandpa was grieving and didn't notice that my brother and sister were terrorizing me. He probably didn't know how to handle my mother's worsening alcohol addiction either.

Two years later, my grandpa died, and with him went the last friend I had. I withdrew into a fantasy world where everything was peaceful and colourful. I told my stories to the neighbour's cat, which earned me the nickname 'Ignatia', a nod to the priest who preached to the birds, when my brother caught me during one of my storytelling sessions.

3. No roses without thorns

Every Saturday, I had to go to the market to buy groceries: cookies, vegetables, eggs, and, strangely enough, flowers too. Why did my mother want flowers when she didn't even look at them? When I got home from the market, I would pull the wilted flowers out of the old bouquet and bring the remaining ones to my bedroom. The little bouquet brought colour to the evenings I spent in my room. I would put the new flowers in a vase on a messy side table in a corner of the living room by the window.

I didn't mind buying flowers. A handsome boy was running the flower stall. He was about 16 years old, a little older than me. He was always very nice. Once, he gave me an extra flower, a rose.

"A special one for you," he said.

I blushed. I wasn't used to receiving compliments. I dreamed the entire week about the flower boy. Instead of doing my homework, I sat on the side of my bed with the rose in my hands. The sweet smell brought back the memory of that special moment when he smiled at me and our fingers touched for a brief moment. I could hardly wait to go to the market again. Was it possible to finally have a friend again? It had been so long since Grandma died. I would have been so happy to call her and tell her about him.

The next Saturday, I bought the other groceries first before heading over to the flower stall. I had to wait a long time for my turn at the vegetable stall. I restlessly peered through the shoppers to look at the flower boy. He was always busy. No wonder; the bouquets he arranged were beautiful. Finally, it was my turn and I bought the vegetables on my shopping list.

I left the lineup in front of the vegetable stall and headed to the flower boy.
What I saw next made the blood drain from my face. I couldn't believe my eyes. At the flower stall stood a girl with long blonde hair. She accepted a flower from the flower boy, stood on her tiptoes, and kissed him on the cheek. That wasn't even the worst; he embraced her and kissed her back full on the mouth.
I turned my head and walked lightheaded past his stall. When I got home, I threw the rose and the old bouquet in the compost bin. From then on, I bought my flowers from the old lady who had her stall beside the music tent.

My brother, sister and I spent the weekends at my father's. He lived with his girlfriend in a house they were always renovating. It was never-ending. As is often the case, a painter lets the paint of his house peel off, or a gardener lets his garden turn into a jungle. It took my father years to renovate his house. He always helped other people first because they paid him.
At first, his girlfriend Barbara accepted this way of life. As the years dragged on and they still stumbled over loose planks and nails, the unfinished projects increasingly became the cause of their fights. When they bought the fixer-upper and just moved in with each other, it seemed very romantic to camp out in the shed. It wasn't a problem at all because it was summer. Before they even noticed, in their honeymoon euphoria, it was winter. It became more and more difficult to keep each other warm at night, no matter how much they cuddled.
They placed a woodstove in the middle of the shed, which was supposed to keep the space warm. Every time Barbera would leave for work or shopping, the fire would dwindle or

die. When she returned, a light frost had covered their belongings. She thought it was an impossible situation and urged my father to, at least, fix the kitchen and the bathroom as soon as possible. He did, and the rest of the work dragged on at a very slow pace. After 15 years and a lot of yelling, the renovation of the house was pretty much done.

Barbara had nothing to complain about anymore, now that the house was finished. The jobs on their to-do list had become their only topics of conversation. Barbara got bored and decided to try another man. One day, she moved in with a good friend of my father's.

My father fumed with rage and called her a bitch. I looked at him when that word blasted out of his mouth, and I knew that he knew what I thought. He stared at me, grabbed a vase from the coffee table, and hurled it at me. I ducked, and the vase shattered the window. It landed with a clunk on top of the barbeque, breaking into shards. It was the same barbeque that had been used at my father's business party the previous Saturday. This particular friend had attended the party, too.

"History repeats itself," I couldn't help but say out loud.

My father's face turned red, and he shouted, "You should never have been born."

Hearing those words spoken out loud by my father, hit me hard.

For the first time, my sister and I spent the weekend at my father's house without my brother. A hostile atmosphere blanketed the house. My father slammed the doors, fixed the window, and beat the crap out of the barbeque. With a force like a high-speed express train, he finished all the remaining major projects in his house.

I started counting the days until I reached the legal age of 19 and could leave my family. My brother had just turned 19 and moved into his own apartment that same week. The image of the piles of dishes and laundry haunted me. I was determined never to set foot on his doorstep.

Now that my brother had moved out, my sister was less hateful. We didn't become friends, but the atmosphere was bearable. My mother became increasingly overweight and spent her days glued to the television. I kept the house clean while my sister chased after boyfriends, acting like a slut. Sometimes she would bring a boy home and spend hours with him in her bedroom. My mother didn't notice anything, but the sounds coming from my sister's room, apart from the heavy metal music, made me nauseous.

4. Graduation party

Around my 16th birthday, I got a job restocking shelves at the local supermarket.

"Can't you find something better?" growled my father when he heard about it.

"No," I said, "I like doing it."

"Like doing it," he snorted, but he left it at that. After all, he was happy not to have me hanging around the house every Saturday.

I didn't make much money at the job, but anything I was able to save, I put in the bank. I didn't tell my mother about my job. I was afraid she would take my money away. I wasn't concerned about my father; he didn't care for money. Slowly but surely, I saw my funds grow, and with that money came the hope for a better life.

In the meantime, I did my best in school. I avoided everything that could cause trouble with my parents and possibly result in the loss of my Saturday job. That job was my way out of a poisoned home where my mother wandered around like a no-good loser and my sister behaved like an animal. It was my only road to freedom. I needed patience. Time and money were my friends.

Finally, my graduation came in sight, along with my 19th birthday.

"Dad, may I have some money to buy a dress for the graduation party?" I asked him at the last minute.

"That too, eh?" he grumbled, but despite his lack of enthusiasm, he gave me a couple of hundred dollars.

I began my search on the Internet for a secondhand dress. I also visited every thrift store in town, and I got lucky. I found a cobalt blue dress for only fifty dollars. The dress beautifully matched my cognac-coloured hair and blue eyes. At a big shoe store, I bought the cheapest shoes I could find in my size. I also found fashion jewelry to match my dress. I didn't want to gamble on borrowing makeup from my sister, so I bought mascara and rouge. I didn't need much makeup; my freckles gave my face enough colour. Getting an updo wasn't an option, but I wasn't worried about that. My hair naturally curled and fell in beautiful locks on my shoulders.

The rest of the money I deposited into my bank account.

My father was the only family member who came to the graduation ceremony. My mother pretended to be sick, and my brother and sister, apparently, weren't able to get the time off work. I thought it was perfect.

My father joined me in the lineup of waiting classmates and their parents. When it was my turn to go into the auditorium, he offered me his arm, and we walked down the aisle to the front. I had the feeling a bride must have, seeing a new future waiting for her at the end of the aisle.

In the evening, at the dinner organized by the school, my father and I were placed at the same table as Pete's family. Pete was, just like me, a loner in school. I understood why the graduation organizers placed us together.

The class dean led us in prayer. He thanked God for His good care during the past years. Suddenly, tears welled up in my eyes when I realized how God had always taken good care of me despite the fact I grew up in a broken family. For the first 11 years of my life, I had a loving grandpa and grandma, and although I didn't have friends in school, school had been a safe place for me.

After the prayer, the dean gave us riddles. The students who gave the correct answers got permission to go first, with their family and friends, to the buffet table to fill up their plates.

"What are you going to do when the holidays are over?" asked Pete, who sat beside me.

"I'm going to travel as soon as I'm 19," I told him in confidence. I leaned towards him a little so my father wouldn't hear what I was about to say. "Nobody in my family knows yet, so I hope you'll keep your mouth shut."

He looked a bit scared because of my sharp tone but then he started to smile.

"Can I come with you?" he whispered.

I looked at him, surprised. "Why?" I asked.

"For the same reason as you?" he said. "Just to get away from my family?"

"How do you know that's what I want?" I replied.

"My brother," he said, while directing his eyes across the table towards him, "was flirting with your sister for a couple of weeks. He told me it's a mess at your place."

"What," I burst out. "A mess? Am I not doing enough to keep the house clean?"

"No, no," he apologized. "I mean that you guys, just like our family, are not a real family but only stick together because you don't know what else to do."

I calmed down a bit.

"What are you planning to do after the holidays?" I asked him.

Again, he looked around the table warily and said almost inaudibly, "My father wants me to work in his sand and gravel business delivering soil to customers. Delightfully boring," he added.

"What would you like to do instead," I asked him in an equally soft voice.

"I want to paint," he said, "but they're all laughing at me. 'You can't make a living doing that,' they say."

"You can, if you're good," I said passionately.

He shrugged. "I think so too. And you, what would you like to do?" he asked.

"I want to write, but you can't make a living doing that," I said, and then we both burst out laughing.

Suddenly it got quiet around the table, and when I saw the surprised looks of our table companions, I realized that this was maybe the first time our families had heard us laugh. I stared into the eyes of Pete's brother until he looked away and started poking at the peas on his plate with his fork. Pete's mom looked back and forth from Pete to me. She smiled slyly. I knew what she was thinking: she might be the right fit for our Pete.

Well, I thought, forget it.

I glanced sideways and saw that Pete was focused on his food too. He actually was a nice guy. He had brown hair that fell partly over his forehead. He always had a shy, kind look in his eyes.

"Are you going to the afterparty?" asked Pete after dinner.

"Nah," I said.

"Let's go together," he suggested.

"They don't even want us there," I protested.

"I don't care," he said.

I looked at him, surprised. He was full of unexpected twists.

"Okay," I said slowly.

My father was good with that. He was already glad he didn't have to think about me anymore. He'd had a few too many beers and staggered to his pickup truck.

The afterparty was as I imagined it would be. Lots of squeals and giggles from the girls. The parents of a girl in my class made their house available for the party, and we were allowed to use the swimming pool and the hot tub. A bonfire was lit. Pete and I roasted marshmallows stuck on long, thin branches. We ate from the same bag of chips.

"Hey," mocked a classmate walking by behind us. "You're a nice couple. You figured that out a little late now that it is the end of the school year."
Pete and I looked quietly at him, unimpressed. Uncomfortable, he raised his hands in apology and walked away as fast as he could.
We looked at each other, smiled, and gave a high five.

5. That black thing

I worked the whole summer as a shelf stocker at the supermarket. With the money I made, I bought a Samsung Galaxy tablet and a telephone to stay in contact with Pete. My sister seldom let me use the PC in our living room. Although it had cost me a pretty penny, I was happy with my purchase. I got a new e-mail address, created a Facebook account, and set my privacy settings at the highest possible level. I turned down all the friend requests I received. Pete was the only one I added as a friend. We messaged each other every day, and our plan to leave for the West Coast began to take shape.

I started on the story I wanted to write and tried to piece together some poems, but they didn't give me enough freedom for the lengthy descriptions that were swirling around and around in my head.

It took me quite some time to come up with a password nobody would guess, to ensure no hacker would invade my computer. I hid my tablet under my mattress when I couldn't take it with me, but normally, it lived in my bag. At work, I hid my bag. I didn't want anybody to find out my thoughts and what I had written down.

It was a relief to finally pen all the stories that had been piling up in my brain. Page after page, I typed them out. I became anxious about what would happen if my tablet got stolen or broke down. I bought a USB stick and copied my stories onto it. I hid the USB stick in my toiletry bag, which I took with me to my father's house. I thought it was better if the stick stayed at his place, and I found a good spot in an unfinished part of the wall in my bedroom.

Until one Friday evening, when I came home and saw that the wall had been redone with new 2 x 4s. My knees felt like they had turned to Jello. My father had, for sure, found my USB stick. He could have read everything on it by now.

I went to the living room, where he was sitting at the table reading the local newspaper, and said, as nonchalantly as possible, "I see you finished the wall in my room really nicely."

"Yes," he muttered, while he continued reading. "I found a black thing that people use in a computer. It's yours, I guess? It's in the kitchen on the counter."

He didn't look up from his newspaper, and I hurried into the kitchen. Indeed, there was that 'black thing'. I snatched it up. I called, in a shaky voice, to the living room, "I got it. Thanks!" I added, "My room looks really neat."

I didn't expect an answer, but he said, "You're welcome."

I felt light as a feather when I walked up the stairs. I stood in front of the bedroom window and stared over the flat landscape behind my father's house. The sun slowly started its descent.

Was that my father who gave me that answer? Was it possible people could change? That miracles exist? "Thank You, Lord," I said softly.

6. Preparations

Slowly, the summer came to an end. Bit by bit, I collected all the things I needed for my trip to the mild climate of Canada's west coast: a big backpack, various camping gear, and non-perishable food. It couldn't be too heavy because I wasn't that strong. Pete was also busy collecting supplies, and we kept each other updated online. I hid the items in the shed on my father's property.

There was one more week to go before I turned 19. Just by chance, something went wrong at Pete's place that same week. Pete's father fell ill and wasn't able to work. Pete was the only other employee in the sand and gravel business, so his father's work was added to his plate too. It didn't seem likely that his father would be better before the end of the week and return to work.

I had the choice to wait until Pete could come with me or go ahead without him in the hope that he could join me later. Going by myself meant I would have to buy the supplies Pete would have brought with him. It would have been easier for me to purchase Pete's items, but it would leave him in a predicament once he was able to leave.

"Hey Pete," I messaged him on Facebook, "I want to leave Saturday, the day before my birthday, just as we initially planned. Please come with me!"

"I'm afraid it's not going to work," his reply came back. "My father is too sick to leave his bed."

"Is there nobody who can take over your work?" I tried.

"Not that I know of. We're not going to place an ad because we hope this situation is temporary."

"Do I really have to go by myself?" I begged.

"No, you don't. Just wait until I can come with you. Stay a little longer. It's dangerous for a girl to travel by herself."
"That's it! Come with me!"
"Nadia, stop! Have a little patience."
"You told me your family isn't always so nice to you. Now you have to be nice to them? I'm so fed up with this. Just come, would ya? Your parents will find somebody else to take over your work."
"No, I'm not coming right now," came his resolute answer.
I felt frustration and anger bubble up inside of me. I gritted my teeth.
"I'm leaving Saturday night," I wrote firmly.
"Okay," he replied.
I stared at the screen. Was this the only thing he had to say? I threw a pencil across the room. It disappeared into the open closet and landed softly among my clothes.
"Useless action," I scolded myself under my breath.
A new message appeared on my screen.
"I don't want to abandon my parents. I don't want to return evil with evil."
I sighed and gave in. Of course, he was right. To make problems worse just to get what you want was also a useless action.
"You're sweet," I wrote hesitantly.
It took a while before his answer came back.
"Thank you, :-), you sometimes too :-)."
Despite not getting the result I wanted, I had to smile.
I shopped at thrift stores every spare moment I had. During one of my hunts, I found a camouflage print tent and camping cookware.
Nobody ever remembered my birthday because it was still the summer holidays. That was convenient at the moment. As usual, I would stay the weekend at my father's place. I had

saved enough money to pay for the whole trip to the west coast if I went by train. I would be able to survive a couple of months on the remaining savings.

I decided to take the train for the first part of the trip and then hitchhike the rest. At least that way I would be gone before they could try to find me.

"Pete, can you please bring me to the train station in Saskatoon?" I asked him on Facebook. "The train will leave around 10.30 p.m."

"Will do," Pete promised. His family members wouldn't ask where he was going on a Saturday night.

On the weekend, nobody hinted at my upcoming birthday. Deep inside, something cried but I ignored the feeling. Tonight, as soon as the train left the station, my life here would be behind me. I would be on my own. I knew how to take care of myself, how to work for a boss, and I had money to survive for a while.

At 9.30 p.m., Pete drove his pickup truck up the driveway. My father was out with his friends, and I didn't expect him to come home soon. We loaded my backpack into the back of the truck and drove to the train station. I looked at my phone repeatedly to see if there was a text message from the railroad company about when the train was going to arrive. The train was early, which gave the passengers plenty of time to board. I said goodbye to Pete.

"Thank you very much," I said, "you have my e-mail address, Facebook, and telephone number, right? Let me know when you're leaving."

Pete nodded. "I hope my father gets better soon so I can take the chance and leave. In the meantime, I have to stock up my backpack with the missing items," he grinned.

I thanked him again. "I like that we have become friends," I said, feeling a bit shy. A sheepish smile appeared on Pete's face. Then he said, "I think it's awesome."

I climbed the stairs onto the train. Pete handed me my backpack.

Suddenly, he stepped onto the train, wrapped his arms around me, and held me against his chest. He smelled like soil, which comforted me. As quickly as he had embraced me, he let me go and jumped off the train onto the platform. His hands in the pockets of his jeans, he pulled up his shoulders and stood there smiling like a shy teenager. I was going to miss him.

7. The train trip

I dragged my backpack through three train cars to my berth. The berth I had a ticket for was in one of the last cars. I put my baggage on one of the seats. A cool breeze blew in through the open window. I inhaled deeply, and a grin spread across my face. I had taken the first step toward freedom. From now on, nobody was going to control my life anymore. Finally, I was my own boss. No more nasty comments, no more accusing faces. I was free! Only one more day, actually, just another hour and a half, and my parents would no longer have authority over me anymore.

One last passenger dragged a big suitcase on squeaking wheels through the aisle. I heard the whistle of the conductor. A nervous, lighthearted feeling hit me. Slowly, the train started to move. I looked through the window and saw the platform with people waving goodbye. We rolled by, and I searched the platform. Pete was standing in the group, too. I waved.

Right away, I dropped my hand. The doors to the waiting room swung open, and none other than my father walked out onto the platform. I ducked under the window. How was it possible that he knew I was on this train? All kinds of scenarios popped up in my head. The next stop was Biggar, and the train was scheduled to pull out from Biggar at midnight. If my father decided to follow me, he could easily beat the train to Biggar. Around this time of night, the roads would be clear, and knowing him, he would be driving like crazy.

Cautiously, I peeked through the window. In the distance, I saw him following the train with his eyes. He turned around and marched off the platform. I grabbed a young attendant and asked if he could transform my seat into a bed. He went to work right away. My bed was barely finished when the lights of the Biggar train station came into sight. We had arrived way before midnight.

I pulled one of the sheets from my bed and made a makeshift curtain that I hung over the window. I closed the curtain to the aisle, pulled the covers over me, and my toque down to my eyes. I wondered how long the train was going to stay there. I couldn't endure the heat under the blankets for much longer.

Secretly, I snuck a peek through the window. I thought my heart was going to stop beating. On the platform stood two police officers. My thoughts were racing. It would be super easy for them to figure out where my berth was. All I could do was hide and try to avoid them for at least half an hour.

I took my handbag, which contained my tablet, telephone, and important papers, and walked away from my berth. In the hall, where people board the train, I ran into the officers. They had a piece of paper in their hands with a photo on it. I recognized the photo from my graduation. In that picture, my hair hung loose around my face.

I avoided eye contact with them and continued walking while trying to look as relaxed as possible. As soon as I was out of their sight, I snatched my toque from my head, took a hair elastic out of my pocket, and tied my hair up in a high ponytail. I put my toque back over my hair. I walked away quickly and as far as possible from the officers.

I entered the bar car, where people were still sitting at the tables even though it was almost midnight. Of course, I could sit at a table too, but then it would be too obvious that I was a passenger. No, I had to try to blend in with the staff to avoid detection.

A waitress approached me and asked if I wanted a seat.

"No," I said slowly, "I'm very bored. I was wondering if I could help out here."

She looked at me and, to my surprise, said, "Yes, I think that's possible. Hunter isn't feeling very well, so you can sub for her until she's a bit better."

My eyes lit up, and I asked, "What can I do?"

She walked me to the kitchen and told me what needed to be done.

"Hunter is in bed," she said and pointed toward the door at the end of the kitchen.

I saw Hunter's purse on the counter. While the chef was cutting a cucumber into wafer-thin slices and the waitress had returned to the bar car, I took a chance and looked into the purse. I soon found a health insurance card with Hunter's name on it. I would use this if I had to show proof of identification. Luckily, there was no photo on a card like this. I memorized her name and repeated it at least ten times.

In Hunter's purse was a tube of makeup and a mirror. Quickly, I smeared a layer on my cheeks to cover my freckles. The colour was quite dark for my light skin and my freckles disappeared under the layer I applied.

The train hadn't left yet, which meant the officers hadn't given up looking for me. A few minutes later, they entered the kitchen. They greeted the chef and asked if he knew a certain Nadia.

"No," said the chef. He didn't look up and continued to stir an enormous, simmering pot on the stove. I scrubbed a baking sheet until it shone like a mirror.

"May I ask you something?" one of the officers asked, now standing behind me.

"Oh, yes," I said as carelessly as possible. My heart was racing as if it wanted to jump out of my chest, and the pounding in my ears drowned out the sound of the appliances in the kitchen.

"Can I see your proof of identification? Can you please show it to me?" he asked.

"Oh, yes," I repeated.

I dried my hands on the towel that was hanging on the oven door. I walked over to the counter where Hunter's purse was and started rummaging through it. I was buying time because if they were going to question the real Hunter next, I would be in big trouble. The closer to midnight, and thus closer to my birthday, the better the chance I would have that they would leave me alone. I handed Hunter's health card to the officer. He looked at the name on it and gave the card back to me.

Both officers walked to the back door where Hunter was supposed to be. I waited, almost paralyzed by what was coming, but less than two minutes later, they came back, greeted the chef and me, and walked out of the kitchen.

I hurried through the back door to find Hunter. I saw a little room with two beds and another door to a bathroom. In one of the beds was Hunter, buried deep under the sheets. Only her black hair peeked out above the sheet.

"Hey, Hunter," I said, "how's it going?"

She turned towards me, and immediately, I understood why the officers hadn't asked her anything. She was a black girl and didn't have any resemblance at all to the freckled redhead they were looking for. I exhaled, relieved.

"If you need anything, just call me," I said.

"Hmm," she replied, already turning back toward the wall.

For ten more minutes the train stayed put and then finally, slowly, started to move out. Again, I inhaled deeply. I saw that in one more minute, I would be 19. I would never have guessed that my 19th birthday would be so spectacular. Or, better yet, the day before, my own New Year's Eve.

At 12:15 a.m., the bar car emptied as people left for their berths. Not much was left for me to do in the kitchen. I went back to my berth but was still very alert. I hadn't seen the officers leave the train in Biggar because I hadn't been able to look outside from the kitchen.

The aisle to my berth was empty. I walked to my bed as quietly as possible so as not to wake anybody up. Very carefully, I opened the curtain and looked inside. In the dim light coming from the aisle, I saw that my bed was empty. Before disappearing behind the curtain, I looked thoroughly around the train car. Everything seemed very peaceful. The curtains in front of the other berths were closed, though some hung twisted so that I could peek inside from a distance.

When I felt assured that I didn't see any suspicious movements, I sat on my bed. Something under me crunched, and I stood up. There was a piece of paper on the bed. I turned on the light on my phone and saw that it was a note from the police. *Your father is worried. He wants you to contact him.* Underneath was the signature of one of the officers.

What nonsense, I thought. Now, all of a sudden, he is worried?

It didn't make any sense to me. I folded the paper and put it in my handbag. I lay down on my bed and fell asleep to the rhythm of the train. I was vaguely aware of the stops the train made in Unity, Wainwright, and Viking. The next stop would be Edmonton which was my destination. I would no longer be in Saskatchewan but in Alberta. I didn't know if it made a difference to the police what province I was in, but I wanted to minimize my risks and try to keep out of their way.

8. Visiting the pastor

There was nothing frightening to see on the platform in Edmonton. No police officers in sight, looking for teenagers on the run like me. With a black marker, I had written the word 'Vancouver' on a piece of cardboard. I took up position at the exit of the parking lot, holding the cardboard in front of me. Only a few cars were parked. One by one, they drove away. Nobody gave me a ride. A light blue, rusty pickup truck was the last to leave its parking spot and drove to the exit.

I had given up hope of being picked up by anyone. I was trying to come up with a plan B when the beaten-up pickup stopped beside me. The driver's window rolled down. I saw a dark head full of curls appear.

"Hey, Hunter," I said surprised, "how are you doing?"

Hunter observed me with her big, dark eyes. "Are you the girl who subbed for me in the kitchen yesterday evening?"

I nodded, and she said, "Throw your backpack in the back and jump in."

With difficulty, I pushed my backpack over the edge of the pickup bed and walked around to the passenger side to get in.

"Your sign says you want to go to Vancouver, right?" asked Hunter.

"Yes," I confirmed. "Are you going in that direction?"

"I'll drop you off close to Highway 2," said Hunter. "That's where you can get a ride to Calgary."

"Are you going home because you're sick?" I asked.

"I'm going to stay at my aunt's until the train returns from Vancouver, and then I'll get back on it. I live in Toronto."

"Oh," I said. "Is it interesting to work on a train?"

"Yes, it is actually," Hunter nodded. "Especially when police officers come to your bed and ask if you've seen a freckled redhead on the run. At that moment, I hadn't seen her yet. How could I know she was doing dishes in the kitchen?" She burst out laughing.

I wondered how it was possible to be sick and laugh like that. But the laughter was short-lived. Hunter shifted from laughing to coughing and grabbed her stomach.

"I shouldn't do that anymore," she moaned.

"Sorry I used your makeup," I said when Hunter had recovered from the coughing attack. "I had to cover my freckles."

Hunter looked at me. "You shouldn't do that, eh? They suit you very well."

I didn't know how to answer, so I just smiled.

"And sorry," I continued, "that I used your health card as proof of identification."

Hunter looked at me and started laughing again until tears rolled down her round face. I didn't know if they were tears of pain or that she thought it was such a good joke.

She gave me her telephone number and dropped me off at a spot along the highway. I waved at her as she drove away. A big smile appeared on my face. The weather was beautifully sunny, and I felt renewed. The grey atmosphere from home was becoming a distant memory, and a new, unknown future that I was looking forward to, awaited me. Life was good.

I placed my backpack on the ground, held up the thumb of my right hand, and held my 'Vancouver'-sign in my left. Was I begging now? Was I making people feel guilty when they saw me standing here? Was I attracting creepers and serial killers to pick me up?

I stuck my hand in my pocket to make sure my somewhat big, sharp pocket knife was still there. The knife gave me a bit of a calmer feeling. You never knew. The world was full of lunatics, my father always said. How much truth was in that? I had yet to find out. I hadn't been away from home much, and sometimes my father himself was a lunatic. Could I actually believe him?

The waiting felt like forever. My legs grew tired. I sat down on the emergency lane railing. My thighs got cold from the contact with the metal. I stood up. My shoes pinched, and I bent down to loosen my laces. My sign leaned against my knees. It fell with the letters facing the ground. Quickly, I picked it up. I stood up straight again. For a while, I didn't hold up my thumb anymore. With both hands, I held the sign in front of me. I stuck my thumbs in the loops of my belt so my hands and arms could rest.

Finally, a dark grey SUV pulled over and stopped. The window on the passenger side rolled down, and a man in his forties leaned over the passenger seat. He looked kindly at me over his glasses.

"Throw your backpack in the trunk," he said. "It's open."

I did as he said. I got in the car beside him. He asked me where I was from and where I was going.

"How old are you, actually?" he asked a little later.

I burst into laughter. "That's an impolite question," I joked, "you're not supposed to ask a lady her age."

He laughed, too. "You must be a brave lady, going on a trip all by yourself. Aren't you afraid?"

"No, not really," I said as casually as possible. Was it a lie or a half-truth?

Then he became serious. "You have to be careful, eh? The world is full of lunatics."

I stared at him wide-eyed and said slowly, "Okay…"

He told me he was a minister at a church in Edmonton.

"What's your opinion about the Christian faith?" he asked, interested.

"I have good memories of my grandpa and grandma. They always went to church on Sundays. When I was there during the summer holidays, I always went with them. I liked the stories told in Sunday school."

He nodded. "Good."

I didn't tell him that it was a church with mostly old people and that the Sunday school class doubled when my brother, my sister, and I visited.

"Would you like to come to my house for breakfast?" he asked. "My wife would love to have you over."

Hmm, I thought, why not? I've all the time in the world as long as I get to Victoria before winter. I had made the capital of British Columbia my final destination. The winters over there seemed very comfortable compared to the rest of Canada.

"Okay," I said, "I'd love to."

A little later, we pulled into his driveway. It was a two-story, white house with stairs at the front leading up to a porch. On the porch was a table with wooden chairs, and the smell of the red geraniums in the pots on the floor filled the air. A couple of hanging baskets filled with pink and purple petunias hid the porch from the street traffic that drove by. I left my backpack in the car. I would take it with me when I left.

The minister's wife was indeed happy to see me. "I'm going to make coffee right away," she said.

She made a delicious breakfast of eggs and bacon and brought it to the porch where she showed me a chair.

"Would you like to come with us to church?" she asked after breakfast was done.

I felt sleepy, but I was up for anything different from the usual, and I said yes.

We were half an hour early for the service. I looked around a bit in the foyer of the church. Slowly, people trickled in and started talking to each other.

A couple of older ladies asked my name. "You're very welcome," they said. That sounded new and nice.

In the sanctuary, a worship team was practicing for the service. I walked inside and sat in a pew halfway down the aisle. There was a red carpet on the floor. At the front of the church was a window with stained glass. The sun shone through it and poured blue and red rays over the pulpit.

The four members of the worship team varied in age from 15 to 30. Surprised, I listened to their music rehearsal. I didn't know young people were interested in church services. They played for five more minutes, then called it quits. They jumped laughing from the podium and walked down the aisle.

One of the guitar players stopped at my pew.

"Hey, are you new here?"

I nodded.

"Come," he said, "let's go grab a drink."

I stepped out of the pew, and he gave me a hand.

"I'm Jack," he said and started chatting sociably as we walked to the fellowship hall. He offered to pour me a coffee. I turned it down.

"I already had coffee at the minister's house this morning," I said.

I told him the pastor had picked me up from the highway where I was standing in the hope somebody would give me a ride. Of course, he then asked where I was from and where I was going.

"I'm from Saskatoon, and I'm going to Victoria," I told him.

"Cool," he said, "I hope you have a good trip." He put his empty coffee cup on a table. "Let's go back to the sanctuary. The service is about to start."

The church was buzzing with people who were standing and sitting in small groups.

"Come, sit with us," Jack invited me.

He sat down in one of the front rows, and more young people joined us. They looked at me curiously, and I answered them with a shy smile.

Jack and his team stepped on the podium, and the service started. This wasn't the same as the service in my grandma's church. There were only hymns sung by older voices, led by the piano, which gave me tears in my eyes and goosebumps on my arms. The pastor's sermon always slid off me. Here, everybody stood and sang loudly, led by electric guitars, drums, and keyboard rhythm.

I looked around and saw that many people moved to the music. Sometimes I even heard shrill whistling. The joy was contagious. I felt myself carried along by the music. The lyrics of the songs were displayed on a big screen in front of the church. I started to sing, too. I didn't know the melody, but soon I got the hang of it.

The pastor held a beautiful sermon based on the painting 'The Chess Players'. He showed the painting on the screen. The devil sat with a young man at the table on which a chessboard lay. The young man was losing the game. An angel stood at the end of the table, watching. The pastor spoke about a famous chess player who saw the painting. After he studied the chessboard in the painting, he came up with a winning solution for the young man. In short, the story boiled down to the idea that with every choice you make in life, you should think about the consequences. Every well-thought-out choice strengthens your position against the attacks of the devil.

The story inspired me. I actually could win life's game as long as I made the right decisions. I was aware that there would always be circumstances that would influence my decisions. I intended to be cautious and not to take hasty steps. If I just would be careful enough, everything would be alright.

The rest of the day was filled with visits to friends. The pastor and his wife had me in tow for the whole day. During one of the visits, we met John. He was a broad-shouldered, rough guy with an untamed beard.
"Tomorrow I'm driving to Banff and Jasper. Would you like to come with me?" he asked when he heard I was traveling west.
"Sure," I said happily surprised.
The whole weekend was one accumulation of good moments. I savored it. The pastor's wife insisted I stay the night over at their house. I couldn't resist. I had the feeling that I already knew her and the pastor better than I knew my own family. In any case, they had given me more love this one Sunday than I could remember receiving from my own family during my whole life.
"I'm leaving at 6 a.m. I'll pick you up at the pastor's house," said John.
"Fantastic," I said.
John had a nice wife and cute twins, and he was a friend of the pastor. I was pretty sure it would be okay to travel with him.
At night in my bed, I couldn't help but think about everything that had happened so far. I could only conclude that I was a lucky duck. I had no idea how the rest of my trip would be, but so far it was not disappointing at all. I was surprised at how easygoing I was with the people I had met. Building relationships hadn't been my strongest trait. It made me

realize that the pressure my family at home put on me must have been very intense.

9. Beautiful Banff

John parked his Jeep the next morning in front of the house. He knocked on the door. The pastor's wife came down the stairs in her housecoat and opened the door for him.

The pastor stayed in bed. He said goodbye to me the evening before.

"Here," he said, handing me his business card, "in case you ever want to call us."

"Good morning, everybody," John mumbled through his beard.

He picked up my backpack from the hall and, with one easy swing of his arm, let it land in the back of his Jeep like it was a light feather.

"Come with me to the kitchen," the pastor's wife said to me. "I packed something for you for the trip."

She handed me a package wrapped in aluminum foil, which was enough food for breakfast and lunch.

I thanked her wholeheartedly for all the delicious food she had prepared and for the safe shelter she had given me. "I've had an unforgettable weekend," I assured her.

"Come again someday," she said.

She gave me such a firm hug that I could hardly breathe. I felt her well-meant love right through it. She stayed on the porch, waving, until she couldn't see us anymore.

John owned sports and outdoor stores in Calgary, Banff, and Jasper. He talked non-stop about hunting trips he had made with his friends in the mountains around Banff and Jasper. The hunting season had just opened, and he already had several trips planned. He was a guide and took people on his trips. He talked about the bears and cougars he had shot.

"The log house I live in with my family," he proudly told me, "is full of bearskins on the floors and at least ten deer antlers are hanging on the walls."

I imagined a log house decorated with warm wood colours. I saw a woodstove with black bearskins in front of it, where you could lie down with a book in your hands. John would be roasting a piece of deer meat, and the smell would drift into the living room, making my stomach rumble from hunger. That made me think about the package the pastor's wife had given me. I took it out of my bag and opened it.

"The pastor's wife is famous for her cooking skills," said John when he smelled the food.

"Would you like a sandwich with egg, bacon, and cheese?" I asked.

"Yes, please," he said. "My wife never does anything like that for me so early in the morning." It came out with a hint of disappointment.

I tried to make him feel better. "She probably has other good qualities."

He mumbled something, and when I looked at him, not understanding, he said, "She is not too happy that I'm away from home so much. She wants me to spend more time with her and the twins. It's a bit hard to divide my time between my family, my work, and my friends. She has all the time in the world," he added somewhat bitterly. "She doesn't work and is at home the whole day."

I jumped up as if I had just been stung by a wasp. "She doesn't work and is at home the whole day?" I repeated. "Is that not a job, doing the housekeeping? Now," I continued passionately, "At home, I've always been used as a slave. I had to do the housekeeping for four people, do my homework, and work a part-time job. Housekeeping is a lot of work," I said furiously, glaring at him. "Shopping for groceries, washing and folding laundry, ironing clothes, doing dishes, scrubbing floors, dusting, cooking food, washing windows, bringing kids to school, helping with homework," I ranted.

I stopped to breathe. "And," I said, hesitating a bit, "then she also has to be a mate, if you understand what I mean."

He looked at me and grinned. "That's not terrible, eh? That's the fun part."

I was quiet and felt my blood rising to my head. I was so mad I couldn't find the right words. I stuttered, "Now, you know when you have been busy the whole day, I can't imagine that it's fun to have to share the bed with a sweaty guy."

Oops, I thought, did I say that all out loud?

Beside me, it was quiet for a moment, but then John burst out in laughter. That made me even more mad, but I wasn't able to say anything reasonable. Suddenly, the laughter was gone, and John became serious.

"I think you're right," he admitted. "I babysat once when my wife was gone to a conference, and I was very happy that she took the helm again the next day."

We sat in silence for a moment.

"I'll be more understanding with her," he said then.

I didn't answer but stared through the window. So, that existed too; that men admitted they had to improve their behavior. Slowly, it dawned on me what a limited picture I had of men-women relationships in the world.

The road from Calgary to Banff offered a variety of landscapes. The first part was flat, with endless dry grasslands on both sides of the road. As we drove further, more pine and fir trees began to appear. In the distance, we could see the Rocky Mountains and the landscape became more rolling.

John was a great travel guide. He told me about the sites of interest we were passing through. Just before we drove into the mountains, we saw a sign for Stoney Indian Park.

"The Stoney First Nations have the moniker 'Cutthroat'," told John.

"Are they cutting people's throats?" I asked, horrified.

"In the earlier days, probably, but not now. Otherwise, I would have heard about it," John grinned. "They got the name 'Stoney' from white explorers. They cooked broth on hot stones in bowls made of hides."

We reached the Rockies. Along the highway, high, steep mountains rose. At about a hundred-kilometre drive from Calgary, we drove through the town of Canmore in the Bow Valley.

"Canmore was one of the locations during the Calgary Olympics in 1988," John shared with me. "This was the place for the cross-country skiing and biathlon competitions."

"How do you know all of this?" I asked.

"You are a guide, or you are not a guide," said John, shrugging. "Don't forget to look at the 'Three Sisters'. He pointed to three mountain peaks towering high and sisterly beside each other above the town.

Just before we reached Banff, the highway split into four lanes. In the middle of every lane stood a tollbooth where vehicles stopped to pay.

"With the money they're raking in here, the parks and trails are maintained," John informed me.

"I think it's fair for tourists to contribute to the costs of maintenance," I said.

"I agree," was John's response.

Upon arriving in Banff, we went straight to John's store.

"You have to entertain yourself for the morning," he said. "I've got business to attend to."

"No problem," I answered.

"Make sure to be back at the shop by noon. Then we'll hit the road again. Give me your phone number so I can call you if I'm done early."

I went shopping on the main street. I enjoyed myself and walked in and out of every store. I behaved and felt like a real tourist. I picked up decorative rabbit pelts to feel them, took knitted sheep wool sweaters from the racks, and put them back again. I took selfies with cowboy hats and took a picture of the majestic mountain standing prominently at the end of the street. The sun shone on the snowy top and the colourful buildings. The sky behind the mountain was clear blue and everything seemed as happy as I felt.

Even the police car, slowly driving down the main street, couldn't dampen my joy. Just in case he was looking for me, I stepped behind a clothing rack that was on the sidewalk. I moved the pieces of clothing back and forth while peeking through the rack, following the car with my eyes. The police officer didn't seem to be looking at anything in particular.

At noon, I was back at John's outdoor shop. He gestured that he needed five more minutes and then would be ready.

"Are you hungry?" he asked when he walked up to me a little later.

"Actually, yes," I said.

"Okay then, I know a restaurant where we'll have a fantastic view of the mountains from the second floor."

We found a spot outside on the sun deck. The view was spectacular. We looked out over the town, with a ring of mountains in the background. The sun glinted on the snow high on the peaks. We ate our lunch and enjoyed the view.

After finishing lunch, John paid the bill. "You keep your money in your pocket. You need it for other things," he said, giving his credit card to the waitress.

While he was busy talking to the waitress, I looked at his face. Despite his rough appearance, there was an undeniable kindness in his manner. Did he suspect I didn't want to go home? That I was a runaway and nobody knew where I was at the moment; that they were probably searching for me and were worried, and that Pete would probably like to know how I was doing? Did John know I had no job and no shelter for the winter? What if the winter in Victoria was colder than I expected? Was my sleeping bag warm enough? Was I going to have enough money for food?

I walked behind John down the stairs of the restaurant. Wouldn't it be better to stay here, and ask John if I could work in one of his stores? I quickly abandoned the thought. I was still way too close to home.

"What's your plan?" asked John when we were back on the main street. "Are you coming with me to Jasper, which is two hundred kilometres to the north, or are you going in the direction of Kamloops, via Highway 1 to the west?"

"I would like to see Jasper and Lake Louise," I pondered aloud, "but it's in the wrong direction. I think it's better to go further west."

"Okay, that's good. Get in my Jeep, I'll bring you to the next hitchhiker stop," he said.

He jumped in the car and I followed his example.

"Will you take good care of yourself?" asked John when we said goodbye at the highway overpass. He placed my backpack on the side of the road.

I nodded. "Say 'hi' to your wife. And to the pastor and his wife. And to Jack," I added to the list.

John tilted his head and looked at me from the corners of his eyes. "Jack?" he asked curiously.

"Yes, just Jack," I said a little irritated, "the guitar player in church."

John looked at me mischievously.

"What?" I said fiercely.

"Nothing," he said innocently. "Just for the heck of it, I wondered …"

I shook my head and made a quasi-disapproving face.

"No problem, I'll say 'hi' to Jack too," he said.

"Thank you very much," I said, pretending to be serious. I thanked him wholeheartedly for the ride and the lunch.

"Come here," he said and opened his arms. I disappeared into his hug.

"Thanks for the stories you told me about the interesting sites. I found them very fascinating," I said, smothered in his embrace.

"You're very welcome," he said, jumped into his Jeep, and drove away.

I watched the Jeep until it became a yellow spot in the distance.

10. Tortilla

So far, hitchhiking had been smooth sailing. I hoped to meet more people like Hunter, the pastor, and John. My destination was now Kamloops, which was still quite a distance away. While shopping, I had found a clean, straight piece of cardboard in a garbage can. Now was the right time to write down the name of the next city.

The weather held up nicely. In the clear blue sky were only a couple of clouds. I had been standing along the highway for a while when a semi-truck with a picture of gigantic tortilla chips on the side stopped.

I pulled myself and my backpack up into the cab.

"You can drive with me to Revelstoke," said the young, blonde driver. His arms were covered with tattoos, which I looked at with awe. I placed my backpack on the front seat, between me and the driver.

The salesman on the radio blared, "Come to the Ford dealer and even get cash for your clunker!" The disc jockey announced a new CD from a well-known pop group.

We drove back onto the highway. It wasn't long before I started shifting back and forth, somewhat uncomfortable in my seat. Should I start a conversation or not? The driver's indifference felt awkward.

"Do you like being a truck driver?" I asked. I had to bend and look around my backpack to see him.

"You have to do something to make a living," he said, shrugging.

I agreed. "But wouldn't you rather do something else?"

He looked at me, surprised.

"No," he said, "Anyway, I wouldn't know what else to do."

"Are there not many jobs to find in the area?" I continued.

He looked at me, bored, but still gave me an answer. "It's very busy in the tourist season in places like Banff. But I can't picture myself running around with plates of food in a restaurant or working in a shop where tourists just browse without buying anything."
That reminded me of someone like Nadia from Saskatoon.
"In any case, I get to see something of the area," he said.
Yes, I thought, every day the same route and the same area.
Again, it was quiet, except for the music.
I looked out the window, and after studying fir trees for half an hour we saw a sign for Lake Louise.
"Can we drive by Lake Louise?" I asked.
"I don't have time for that, and I don't want to. Nothing interesting to see there. Just a bluish-green lake surrounded by mountains. I can drop you off here so you can find a ride with somebody else to Lake Louise if you like," he said.
"No, no, it's all good," I said quickly. Who knew how long I would have to wait for another ride?
Too bad, I thought. I had seen beautiful pictures on the Internet. I made a mental note to add Lake Louise to my to-do list for the future.
Again, it went silent.
I risked another attempt at starting a conversation.
"Do you have a hobby?"
"No," he said, "I don't think so. I like watching TV," he grinned.
"But what do you do on the weekend?"
"Oh, I sleep in till around noon, and at night I go with my friends to the pub."
"You don't work on your car, and you don't hunt? I heard that hunting season just opened."

"No, man, that's way too much trouble. I drive my truck during the week and I relax in the evenings and on the weekends."

The radio was once again the only sound besides the monotonous humming of the engine, and slowly I dozed off. I didn't want to keep the conversation going anymore. Without a question from his side, the conversation was a dead end anyway. I was okay with that.

The driver dropped me off at the freight truck parking lot just over the Columbia bridge in Revelstoke. I thanked him for the ride. His workday was done. Tomorrow, he'll head to Highway 23 and drive the same route as he did today. I'm glad it's him and not me.

11. Oh, Boy

I felt exhausted from the dull drive. The joyful morning in Banff seemed so far away. The indifferent atmosphere of home hung over me. When I realized that, I stood up straight and gave myself a good stretch.

"That's in the past," I told myself. "Don't go back to that disappointing, hopeless life."

I spun around on the parking spot where the tortilla driver had dropped me off, and I decided to stay close by for the night.

A lonely dog was scavenging near a garbage can. Friendly brown eyes looked at me when I approached him. I crouched down, and he slowly came closer, sniffing everywhere. His fur was black with a white nose. White fur went up from his nose to his forehead into a narrowing strip. He allowed me to pet him, and I was able to read his collar. It said: 'Boy'.

"Hey, Boy," I said. Immediately, he looked up at me and wagged his tail.

"Poor animal, you're just a loner like me."

I saw little grey hairs on his snout. How old would he be? How could people leave a sweet dog like this behind in a parking lot? It was clear to me that he had been dropped off by travelers.

I hugged Boy. That was the start of our friendship.

With the chips truck, I had driven over the Columbia River bridge. I walked back to the river, with Boy following me. We went down the slope to the bridge's pillars. The cars rushed over our heads.

I sat down by the river, a little away from the bridge. There was enough room to set up my tent for the night. A couple of big freight trucks thundered over the bridge. Despite the noise, I found it comforting to know there were people close by.

I had some leftover lunch the pastor's wife had given me, and I shared it with Boy. Slowly, the bridge traffic decreased, and dusk crept up from the river onto the land. This was the first time since I ran away from home that I would be sleeping outside, alone.

I found a spot at the edge of the woods and took my tent out of its package. There was still enough daylight left to read the manual, and I soon figured out how to set up the tent. I rolled out my sleeping bag and crawled in with all my clothes on. I left the tent door open as long as it wasn't fully dark yet.

Boy walked around the tent and lay down in front of the door under the small awning. Suddenly he stood up, pricked up his ears, and sprinted away. Immediately after that, I heard a lot of growling and shrieking.

I peered into the twilight. Boy was fighting with another animal. It was too big to be a cat. Boy came towards me with the struggling creature in his jaws. The striped tail of the animal lashed back and forth. It fought for its life. I saw the black mask on its face: a raccoon. It tried to free itself, but Boy bit him firmly in the neck and pushed it onto the ground.

Sour pieces of bacon and eggs came up to my mouth. My jaw clenched. I turned my head away, but from the corner of my eyes, I saw the fight continuing. Boy growled wildly and bit the raccoon repeatedly in the neck until it stopped moving.

How uncontrollably cruel nature was. Or was it just the opposite? Was it a controlled cleanup of animals bothering others? Or had the raccoon entered Boy's territory, and so it had to be killed?

After a while, Boy came back to me. He lay down, sighed deeply, and fell asleep as if nothing had happened.

My army-print tent blended in seamlessly with the surrounding greenery. I didn't want to draw attention to myself as long as I didn't know if people were still searching for me. Miraculously, I slept well, maybe because Boy was there, keeping watch over me.

Close to 6 a.m., dawn broke, and I woke up. I decided to break camp at once and move on. I didn't know how long I would have to wait for my next ride. Boy followed me to the freight truck parking lot. I pulled out my 'Kamloops'-sign and went to the exit of the parking lot.

I wasn't standing there long before a heavy truck driver jumped out of his cab. He walked toward me, trying to hoist up his pants. It took him a while to cross the parking lot, but when he was within earshot, he called out and pointed in the direction of his truck.

"Do you want a ride with me?" he called.

With Boy on my heels, I started walking toward him. Why, I don't know, but it felt safer to drive with a trucker than in a random person's car. At least, I told myself, freight trucks drive longer distances, which would get me to my destination faster. This truck was big, and the cabin was shiny blue. The name of an American warehouse was advertised in huge letters on the trailer.

I hauled my backpack up the stairs to the cab and settled into the luxurious passenger seat. Boy found a spot on the floor behind the seats.

"I'll bring you to Abbotsford, and then I'll drop you off," said the driver.

"Good," I said.

That's fantastic, I thought, then I'll be almost in Vancouver; much further than Kamloops!

"My name is Rob, by the way," said the driver.

"I'm Nadia, and that's Boy," I said, pointing behind the seats. Slowly, the freight truck geared up, and we drove to the exit of the parking lot, toward the highway.

"Wow, you're so skilled to operate a giant monster like this," I praised him.

"Thank you," he said. "Most people have no idea how much attention you need to pay to so many things when you're hauling so much weight. Accelerating is slow, but braking also takes time. It's no joke when cars cut in front of you while you're trying to stop at a stoplight. It takes all my strength not to get extremely mad. Luckily, I've never driven into a line of cars."

Rob seemed to be a better conversationalist than my previous driver. Every once in a while, we had a moment of silence, but it didn't bother me.

The highway winded through the mountains. The foliage became more diverse, with low shrubs alternating with broad-leaved trees and conifers.

We stopped at several supermarkets along the way to deliver products. Boy loved to run around outside for a break. I took the opportunity to use the bathroom and stock up on some extra food. I now had to take care of two souls. I bought a metal bowl and some dog food. A collar and a leash would be convenient to have, so I bought those as well.

After more than eight hours of driving, we made our last stop in Abbotsford. I considered crossing the border at Sumas and going to the U.S. but quickly abandoned that thought. That would be asking to be arrested.

12. Warning

The afternoon came to an end, but there was still a chance I could get a ride to Vancouver. I pulled my backpack onto my back and walked to the highway. On the back of my cardboard sign, I wrote: 'Vancouver ferry'. It would be ideal to take the ferry to Victoria, which is in the south of Vancouver Island. But the ferry to Nanaimo, halfway up the island, was a good choice too. From there, I could hitchhike to Victoria.

I started yawning and my legs got tired. Nobody stopped to give me a ride.

I wondered if that was because Boy was with me.

I decided to start walking. I had sat long enough in a truck today. I tied my 'Vancouver ferry'-sign onto my backpack. While I was walking, I held up my left thumb. Boy walked faithfully behind me, sniffing everything that was lying on the side of the road. If he stayed a bit behind because something was interesting to smell, he came running back to shorten the distance between us. When my left arm got tired, I turned around and walked backward so I could use my right thumb.

I walked like that for a long time. Still, nobody gave me a ride. I was afraid I had to find a spot to sleep for the night. I reached the outskirts of Abbotsford and seriously started thinking it was time to stop hitchhiking for the night. Horror stories crept into my head. Dusk was coming and who would still be willing to give me a ride? I could always say 'no' of course, but I didn't know if that was safe either. Some people got mad when you declined their offer for a ride.

It started to rain so I stopped to cover my backpack with a piece of plastic. While I bent over my backpack, which I had placed on the wet asphalt, a car stopped behind me. Happily surprised, I stood up and shielded my eyes from the bright light coming from the headlights. A bright blue and red light on the roof of the car started to flash. The car door opened and slammed shut. Somebody walked around the front of the car towards me.

I didn't say anything. I felt my heart pounding in my throat. That's it, I thought, this is the end of my journey.

The man stood in front of the headlights which helped to cover the glaring lights. I saw dark blue pants with yellow stripes on the sides and sturdy shoes underneath. Slowly, I looked up. I saw a stern face which I didn't want to mess with.

"Good evening, young lady," a deep voice greeted me. "Are you trying to get a ride? I hope you know you're not allowed to hitchhike here."

I shook my head. "I didn't know that," I said, apologizing.

"This will be your only warning," said the deep voice. "If you walk back, you'll find a bed and breakfast on the first street to your left. I advise you to spend the night there."

I nodded timidly, and in the meantime, lifted my backpack onto my back. Slowly I started walking in the direction I came from. When the police officer saw I obeyed his instruction, he stepped in his car and drove onto the highway.

I sighed and followed him with my eyes. My heart was still racing, and my hands were shaking. I let my eyes travel across the darkening landscape. It would have been quite a nice place to set up my tent. Behind the bushes a little further in the field, my camouflage tent wouldn't stand out. I felt torn. Would I dare to go against the advice of the officer or should I walk back and see if the bed and breakfast had a vacancy? My legs hurt, and my backpack leaned heavily on my hips. I wouldn't be surprised if I had raw spots.

"Hey girl, nobody is giving you a ride? What did that officer say?" I heard somebody behind me say.

I turned around and saw a 15-ish First Nations boy on a bike. He rode super slow and balanced dangerously, half on the highway, half on the emergency lane.

"No," I said, "it's not working out tonight. The officer wants me to go to a bed and breakfast." With a wave of my arm, I pointed to the first street on the left.

"Oh, yes," said the boy, "Ruth lives there; her cottage is very nice. Do you have money to stay there overnight?"

I shrugged. "Not really. Do you maybe know a good spot where I could set up my tent? A spot where nobody can see me from the road?"

We stood opposite each other along the highway. The cars driving by splashed mud against my legs. The road shone in the light of their headlights.

"You're not allowed to hitchhike here," said the boy, ignoring my question. "You're only allowed to do that after an intersection. Nobody can stop here to pick you up. Nobody wants to pick up a hitchhiker," he added in a voice like he thought it was strange I didn't know.

"I know," I said, bored.

He was right. The emergency lane was only two metres wide here, and the traffic rushed by. I asked him what I should do.

"Hitchhiking is forbidden west of Golden," continued the boy. "You can get a heavy fine if they catch you."

"Golden?" I asked surprised. "Where is that?"

"Just before Banff, seen from this side," he said.

I realized I had been hitchhiking illegally for the whole day. I was debating between the two choices.

"I don't want to walk all the way to that bed and breakfast just to see that there's a 'no vacancy'-sign hanging there and I still have to find another place," I complained.
"I'll bike over there, okay?" asked the boy.
"Thanks," I said surprised and somewhat relieved. Immediately he turned his bike and disappeared in the darkening evening.
In less than three minutes he was back. "There's no room available there," he panted after the fast bike ride. He looked at me and waited for my decision.
Again, I asked the boy if he knew where I could spend the night. He nodded toward the bushes I considered earlier as a sleeping spot.
I peered along the highway to see if the coast was clear. At that moment, there was a big gap in the stream of traffic so I let myself slide down the steep bank. With my hands, I slowed down my speed. The grass was wet and cold. I waited at the bottom of the bank. The traffic rushed by above me. Nobody stopped and no officer was to be seen. I estimated the distance to the bushes and started walking. The boy bounced down the bank on his bike, bracing himself with his heels to prevent himself from falling.
Boy reached the bushes first. The boy sat on his bike watching me set up my tent. He petted Boy on his head and told me they had a Pitbull at home.
"My dog is always outside in the garden on a leash. He keeps the rats and raccoons away."
Well, yes, of course, I thought sneeringly, they're probably attracted to the garbage piled up around your house.
Suddenly, I thought about my brother. Would his apartment look the same as the First Nations houses?
By the time I finished setting up the tent, it was dark, and the boy had disappeared. Fumbling in the darkness, I settled into

the tent. I commanded Boy to lie down under the awning. In the light from the headlights of the traffic, I saw him turn around a couple of times before he lay down.

I closed the zipper of my tent. Anxiously, I listened for sounds that were different from the steady dripping of the rain and the rush of the highway. I didn't hear anything suspicious. I drifted off but was startled a few times because I thought somebody was at my tent. I peeked through the zipper of my tent door, but I didn't see anything. It was pitch black, and there were almost no cars driving on the highway. It was pouring rain now and, to my consternation, I noticed that the side of my sleeping bag was wet. I heard Boy snorting from under the awning. Nothing was wrong. I needed to pee badly, but because it was so dark and it was pouring rain, I decided to hold it until it was a little lighter out.

Just after six, a glimmer of light came through my tent door zipper and I looked outside. The world was grey and gloomily wet. I crawled out of my tent. My muscles had become stiff from the damp cold. The continuous tossing and turning and the laying in an uncomfortable position on the thin mat hadn't done me much good. I petted Boy on his head and took his snout between my hands. His tail made a drumroll against the canvas of the tent.

I found a spot in the bushes behind my tent, and I came back, relieved. I was shocked to find the First Nations boy standing in front of my tent. He grinned and I wondered why Boy hadn't barked. Either he was an everyman's friend or he just recognized the boy from last night and thought he was safe.

"Good morning," I said as casually as possible.

"Good morning to you too," the boy grinned. Immediately he added, "My uncle is going to Vancouver at 10 a.m. and you can drive with him to Horseshoe Bay, where the ferry terminal to Nanaimo is. He will drive further north, but he can drop you off there."

"Great," I said pleased. "Where will he pick me up?"

"He'll drive by this spot. I told him where you are."

"He will stop along the highway?" I asked, worried.

The boy nodded.

"But he is not allowed to pick up hitchhikers, eh?" I asked again.

The boy shrugged. He gave me a package. "That's for your breakfast," he said.

I thanked him and opened the paper wrapped around the food. In the package were half a dozen big pieces of homemade pemmican cake. I held it under my nose and smelled it. My eyes lit up.

"Thank you," I said once more. "It smells delicious."

He grinned again and biked away.

I sat down under the awning of my tent. I moved over as far as possible so Boy could stand out of the rain. I gave him a piece of the cake. Immediately, he begged for more. He probably tasted the dried meat in the cake. I didn't know if the nuts and berries were good for him, so I left it at that small piece. I took his food bowl out of my backpack and put some dog food in it. That was safer.

I now had time to kill before my pickup at 10 a.m. arrived and I had to be ready at the highway.

I waited as long as possible before folding up my tent, so Boy and I could stay dry. Once in a while, I crawled outside to convince myself nobody could see my tent from the highway. In the tent, I studied the map of Vancouver and saw that the route to Horseshoe Bay ran through the outskirts of the city. We could bypass the hustle and bustle of downtown. Maybe I would be able to see the skyline of the city with its skyscrapers, but, as I was looking at the map, I had my doubts. The highway, heading to the northern part of the city, curved away too much. On the ferry, I would have a better view of Vancouver.

When it was almost time to go, I folded the tent and made myself travel-ready.

13. First Nations stories

Just as I started to wonder if I should return to the highway to hitchhike again, a dark green minivan pulled over and stopped along the road. A robust First Nations man emerged from the vehicle.

"Hey there," he called to the bottom of the bank. "Are you the hitchhiker looking for a ride to the ferry?"

"Yes," I called to the top, "that's me." I smiled, relieved.

I stood up from the dry garbage bag I had spread at the bottom of the bank, gathered my belongings, and began to climb the steep slope. I slipped back several times, grabbing onto the grass and pulling myself up bit by bit. By the time I reached the top, my hands were muddy and my shoes soaked.

The First Nations man opened the back door of his van and lifted my backpack inside. Traffic on the highway rushed by us. Anxiously, I kept an eye on them, half-expecting flashing blue and red lights and sirens to suddenly appear. Nobody showed interest in us.

"Come on," the man encouraged Boy. He petted him on his head and Boy jumped into the van, circling a few times before settling down beside my backpack.

I climbed into the van and waited impatiently until the man joined me. Glancing through the rear window at the approaching vehicles, I noticed none stopped. It took a while for the man to maneuver his overweight body into the driver's seat. Finally, he inserted the key into the ignition and started the engine. Slowly, we merged onto the highway and picked up speed.

I sighed deeply, feeling relieved.

The man grinned at me. "Afraid of the police?" he asked.
I nodded.
"They are stricter here than on the Island. They won't bother you there."
"Oh, I'm glad to hear that," I said sincerely.
It didn't take long before the man started sharing stories, clearly his way of passing on knowledge. First Nations traditions aren't typically written down, and I had never heard someone convey as much knowledge as this man did. He explained that he was an elder of the Chiyakmesh tribe, a First Nations community in Squamish, about fifty kilometres north of Vancouver. He spoke about salmon fishing, describing how they used special dams made of large stones placed in circles in the river. The fish would swim into these dams, making them easier to catch with nets.
Then he fell silent, a sad expression crossing his face.
"What is it?" I asked, concerned by the change in his demeanor.
"Oh," he said. "It's nothing."
He became quiet again.
"Did something bad happen?" I inquired after a minute.
"Yes," he replied, "I would like to tell you, but I don't want to harbour bitterness toward white people."
"What did they do now?" I blurted out, feeling anger rise within me.
Of course, I was aware of the atrocities committed against First Nations people in the residential schools. I glanced at the First Nations man beside me. Had he attended one of those schools? Was he subjected to sexual abuse? Forbidden from speaking his own language? Allowed to see his parents only a couple of months each year? Used as a guinea pig in experiments? I didn't dare ask.
He began speaking again, his voice tinged with sadness.

"In the summer of 2005, nine cars of a freight train derailed, spilling their load into the Cheakamus River. Forty thousand liters of natrium hydroxide poured into the river, burning the skin of over five hundred thousand mature and young salmon, trout, and lampreys, making them vulnerable to diseases that led to their deaths. The birds and land animals that ate the contaminated fish also suffered. People living along the river had to be cautious with their well water. Fishing was prohibited in the Cheakamus and Mamquam Rivers and part of the Squamish River to allow the fish populations to recover. It took five years before we saw signs of recovery."

"I had no idea that happened," I said softly. "That was more than ten years ago. Those years must have been very difficult years for your people."

The First Nations man nodded. After a while, he added, "We still don't understand why the river recovered faster than expected, but we are grateful for it."

We both fell silent as we drove over the Port Mann Bridge spanning the Fraser River. Rows of logs were neatly arranged in the river, waiting to be shipped and processed. A little later, we crossed the Iron Workers Memorial Bridge.

"What a strange name for a bridge," I remarked. "How did it get its name?"

"That's a sad story," the man replied. "In 1959, during construction, several pillars of the bridge collapsed due to an engineering miscalculation. Seventy-nine workers plunged thirty metres into the water. Eighteen of them drowned, likely weighed down by their heavy tool belts. Even a diver searching for bodies met the same fate. The bridge was named in memory of those who drowned and the four others who died during its construction."

"Those people sacrificed their lives to make crossing the river easier for us," I mused. "How difficult it must be for their families when they drive over this bridge."

"Do you think so?" the man asked. "In every profession, accidents happen. Take road workers, for example. Wouldn't their families also take pride in knowing there's a visible reminder of the important work their husbands and sons did? Engineers will always remember their mistakes. But mistakes are meant to be learning experiences, making people more cautious and aware of the responsibility they bear for each other."

I nodded, acknowledging the truth in his words. "Yes," I agreed, "sometimes we have to learn things the hard way."

"Don't forget," the man continued, "those engineers didn't intend for that to happen, and they have been severely punished for their mistake. In some professions, there's no room for error, but nobody is perfect. That's why we should consider forgiveness."

"Forgive?" I questioned. "What if their mistake was due to negligence or pride? If they didn't bother to have someone double-check their work or were too proud to admit their error, that would have been even worse."

The man looked at me thoughtfully. "What if you're right, and it was negligence or pride? If everyone found out, they would face public outrage. People might make their lives miserable. How far should we go in punishing someone? Should they be condemned for life, or should they be given a second chance?"

I had to think about that and then said, "Yes, I think they should be given a second chance to do their job, but they should never bear the responsibility alone for a project like a bridge that so many people depend on."

"Fortunately, nowadays computers make fewer crucial mistakes," I added.

The topic was becoming a bit too heavy for my liking, so I changed the subject, "How would you describe your tribe if someone asked you? What sets your tribe apart from others?"

"That's a good question," the man replied.

He paused to consider and then began describing how his tribe was governed.

"In our tribe, every family has a respected elder. The respect you earn within the tribe is based on how much you contribute to the community, the values you uphold, and the spiritual knowledge you share. Respect for each other and generosity with possessions and knowledge are highly valued. Wisdom and knowledge are passed down orally."

"And of course," he added, "our traditional method of making stone dams to catch fish in the river is emblematic of how our tribe lives."

14. On the ferry

While chatting, we arrived at the ferry terminal in Horseshoe Bay. Thankfully, I could still catch the 3.10 p.m. ferry. I said goodbye to the First Nations man and thanked him wholeheartedly for the ride and for trusting me with stories about his people.

I purchased a ticket at the kiosk.

"Can my dog come with me on the ferry?" I asked.

"Yes, he can," replied the lady behind the ticket window, "he can ride for free, but he must be leashed and sit in a special pet room."

The leash and collar I had bought for Boy came in handy. The cashier directed me to the pet room, which was sparsely furnished with a smooth floor, a few benches, and rings on the walls to secure dog leashes. Boy settled down beside the bench where I sat. There were no other dog owners present, which suited me fine; I needed some time alone. The many conversations over the past few days had left me feeling drained.

I gazed out of the window as the boat began to move, navigating out of the harbour and into the open ocean. The water was a bluish-grey, with occasional white foamy crests on the waves. Strokes of white clouds dotted the crisp blue sky. The rain had cleared, and a few sunbeams danced across the water. In the distance behind me, at the ocean's edge, I spotted Vancouver's silver skyscrapers.

I pulled out my tablet, hoping to get an Internet connection. I wanted to inform Pete of my whereabouts, but I couldn't get the connection to work. I desperately wanted to know if Pete would come to Victoria soon. How was his father doing now? When could Pete continue his journey? Would he even go?

Slowly, it dawned on me that I was heading alone to an unfamiliar city. Ahead of me, I saw an empty void. There would be no one in Victoria to welcome and support me. I didn't know anyone there, nor did I know anything about the city. How long could I manage with the money I had left? Would I find a job and shelter?

What had I started? I broke into a cold sweat. Going back was not an option; my life would be even more miserable than before. I pictured the scornful faces of my mother, brother, and sister before me. They wouldn't miss a chance to call me stupid.

I stood up and paced in front of the large square windows overlooking the ocean. My footsteps echoed hollowly. Boy whined softly, tilting his head, his brown eyes questioning me.

Was I making the right decision?

I felt sorry for myself and lonely. I knew I needed to change my mindset. I sat back down. With a click on the Word icon on my tablet, I opened a blank document. During this two-hour ferry ride, I decided to spend the time writing down my memories, as far back as they went.

I began with memories of my grandparents. I typed tirelessly. It helped. My thoughts delved into the past, momentarily forgetting about the uncertain future.

Far too soon for my liking, we arrived on the other side. The ferry docked at the Departure Bay terminal in Nanaimo.

I reassured myself that there would be more opportunities to write, but I was just beginning to get into the flow.

Having captured all that came to mind, I acknowledged that if I ever wanted to share my story with the world, I would need to edit parts of it to avoid hurting those who had caused me pain. I could still hear Grandma's gentle voice saying, 'Don't repay evil with evil', a lesson she imparted during the times my brother and sister terrorized me.

She was right. I had no intention of writing hateful things that would burden my conscience. Those people weren't worth carrying on my shoulders for the rest of my life. It wouldn't help me heal from my pain either. Like the chess players in the pastor's story from Edmonton, I wanted my future decisions to be well-considered. And if things did go awry, I hoped there would be people like the First Nations man from Squamish, willing to offer me a second chance.

Writing down memories from my youth gave me a sense of control over my life. It was both a chronological account of events and a potential self-help book. I resolved that if I ever let someone else read it, I would omit the self-help section. No one needed to know the depths of my heart.

I saved the document along with the other stories I had previously written.

Upon disembarking from the ferry, priority was given to dog owners and cyclists. I seized the opportunity and hurried as fast as I could towards the exit. My goal was to reach the road before the cars drove off the ferry.

I navigated through the crowd waiting to pick up foot passengers. I pulled Boy along with me, hoping someone might be heading to Victoria, although it seemed unlikely since those travelers would have taken the ferry from Tsawwassen. Most on my ferry were headed further north or only halfway south on the island. Still, I decided to give it a try.

As I reached the intersection splitting north and south, the last cars from the ferry passed by without stopping. It was 5 p.m., and I had three hours until dusk.

Walking past 'The Buccaneer' hotel, I suddenly yearned for a warm shower and a soft bed. I dismissed the thought immediately.

The road ahead seemed endless. Was I even heading in the right direction? I tried to pick up my pace, but my backpack felt as heavy as lead.

Forty-five minutes later, I reached the highway. I was relieved to see a sign pointing toward Victoria.

Crossing over Millstone Bridge, I encountered a red pedestrian light at a busy intersection. Leaning against the stoplight pole, my legs were trembling. The light turned green too quickly, forcing me to continue.

The road descended, and my backpack pushed me step by step down the steep incline. I let my back muscles relax, which resulted in a sharp pain in my lower back. Adjusting my posture, I straightened my shoulders, relieving the pain. I realized it was time for a rest.

Later, I ascended the street at a slow pace as it steepened. My hips were sore from where my backpack had been rubbing. Boy, unfazed by the terrain, sniffed around and explored, covering twice the distance I did.

When I felt like I was at the end of my rope, I spotted The Salvation Army on the other side of the upcoming intersection. I decided to ask them for shelter for the night. Just then, a big white pickup truck pulled up to the traffic light. The driver called through the open passenger window, "Jump in and throw your backpack and your dog in the back."

With my last bit of strength, I tossed my backpack into the truck bed. I lifted Boy and struggled to hoist him up. He felt heavier than ever. Finally, I pulled myself into the truck and shut the door.

"Thank you very much," I managed to say, catching my breath.

I turned towards the driver and my heart skipped a beat. Had I really gotten into this guy's truck? I smiled nervously, trying not to show my fear, though it was probably too late.

"I'm not going to eat you, eh," the man said with a grin, revealing teeth that hadn't seen a dentist in a while. He had a thick black beard and piercing black eyes.

Trying to lighten the mood, I joked, "I don't think I taste very delicious," and laughed awkwardly.

"Hahaha," he replied slowly and sarcastically, "you're definitely the funniest kid on the block."

I regretted stepping into his truck immensely. But wasn't it always the way? When you're exhausted and feel you can't take another step, you seize opportunities without thinking, just to escape misery. I concluded that letting your guard down could be dangerous.

"You can ride with me until the gas station in South Wellington, just past Nanaimo but before the airport," he informed me.

"Okay," I agreed, though I had no clue where that gas station was.

The driver hit the gas when the light turned green, speeding towards the next intersection where cars were waiting. Miraculously, we stopped just in time. My toes curled in my shoes, and I took shallow breaths. A political interview played on the radio, but I couldn't make sense of it. The voices grated on my nerves and added to my confusion.

We left downtown Nanaimo and drove through the outskirts, entering the industrial area where only places like Tim Horton's, Dairy Queen, and McDonald's remained open. Soon, we left that part of the city behind, rushing past closed businesses for the day.

Glancing back at Boy through the rear window, I saw him enjoying the wind, his ears flapping. At the same time, I glanced sideways at the driver. He turned to me sharply.

"Do you know why I gave you a ride?" he asked.

"Hmm, no," I hesitated.

"Because, when it's dark," he continued, "it's not safe along the highway for girls like you."

"Okay," I said slowly. But why would it be safe with him in his truck?

His intense gaze seemed to penetrate my thoughts. "You don't have to be so afraid of me. I'm not going to do you any harm."

I didn't know what to make of someone who spoke so explicitly about danger.

"I'll drop you off near the gas station and show you a place to set up your tent."

"Is that spot safe?" I asked cautiously, realizing he would be the only one who knew where I was.

"Okay, okay, I know I'm intimidating," he said, pulling a business card from his jacket pocket. I accepted it.

"Does that make you feel better now?" he asked. "Now you know who I am. Why did you jump in the truck with someone you're clearly afraid of afterward?"

"I was very tired," I explained. "I walked all the way from the ferry, and I was relieved someone stopped to give me a ride."

"When you're tired, you have to be aware that you might make wrong decisions," he advised.

I nodded unhappily. "I had already come to that realization myself."

For the rest of the ride, Mr. Scary turned out to be much better than I expected. He mentioned having a wife and two young daughters, which eased my concerns somewhat. He dropped Boy and me off unharmed at his sister and brother-in-law's home, situated behind the gas station. He knocked on their door, and his brother-in-law answered.

"This girl," he said, pointing at me, "would like to pitch her tent for the night and stay here."

"Sure, that's fine," the man nodded, eyeing me up and down before closing the door.

Mr. Scary escorted me to a corner of the garden where the woods began. "You can set up your tent over there."

He wished me a good night and success on my journey. Then he returned to his truck and drove off into the dusk, the engine roaring as his pickup truck disappeared from view.

It gave me a strange, safe feeling knowing that people knew I was staying there and were okay with me camping on their property. I quickly set up my tent, fed Boy, ate some of the pemican cake the First Nations boy had given me, and crawled into my sleeping bag. Exhausted, I fell fast asleep.

15. South Wellington

The next morning, I was awakened by a trickling sound on my tent. I unzipped the door and saw that it was drizzling rain, drops falling from the tree branches onto my tent. Shivering, I crawled back into my sleeping bag. Through the open door, I watched as Boy roamed around on the wet grass.

Suddenly, a little boy approached my tent. He came closer cautiously. Boy noticed him too, wagging his tail as he approached. The boy laughed and petted Boy on his back. Boy sniffed at him, and the child winced at the lick Boy gave him on his face. Quickly, he wiped his cheek with the sleeve of his sweater.

From the side of the house, a young woman appeared and approached my tent. I hurriedly jumped out.

"Good morning," she greeted warmly, "did you sleep well?"

I nodded. "Good morning to you too," I smiled, extending my hand. "I'm Nadia."

She shook my hand, her dark eyes observing me with curiosity. Her black hair framed her face in curls, and when she smiled, a row of white teeth appeared.

"I heard from my husband that my brother dropped you off here yesterday," she explained. "I came to see if you need anything."

I shrugged. "No, I don't think so. I have everything I need with me. But thank you for the offer."

"Come inside for a bit," she invited, "I made coffee. Would you like some?"

"Yes, please," I replied gratefully.

I followed her into the house while Boy and the little boy continued their game outside, where the child threw sticks and Boy eagerly fetched them.

"The bathroom is over there," she pointed as we entered. She seemed to understand my immediate need after a night in the cold and wet. I thanked her and quickly used the bathroom, feeling relieved when I returned to the warm kitchen.

Mr. Scary's brother-in-law was seated at the kitchen table, enjoying his breakfast. The little boy had joined him and was sitting on a chair, taking bites of his porridge.

"You can sit here," the woman said, pulling out a chair from the table. She placed a mug of coffee in front of me along with a bowl of porridge. The coffee tasted delicious. I drank half of it quickly, saving the rest for later. Now, I needed to focus on the porridge.

I stirred the mush slowly with my spoon, momentarily wishing I could make it disappear with a magic spell. Realizing that wasn't an option, I cautiously tasted a bit from the tip of my spoon. It was hot and bland.

"Here," the woman said, pushing the sugar bowl towards me, "sprinkle some sugar on it."

She turned back to the counter while the man read his morning paper. I seized the opportunity and added two big spoons of sugar to my porridge, stirring it vigorously. It instantly tasted much better. Glancing up, I saw the man watching me.

"I have a sweet tooth," I apologized.

A faint smile appeared on his face, and he returned to his newspaper. Clearly, he understood my struggle. I managed to eat half the bowl of porridge and washed it down with the remaining lukewarm coffee, all while listening to the lively chatter of the little boy.

After ten minutes, the man stood up, gathered his paperwork and lunchbox, hugged his wife and son, and nodded at me. "Have a good trip," he said to me, and "See you tonight," to his wife before leaving.

"He's not much of a talker," she reassured me.

The little boy placed a drawing in front of me.

"What did you draw?" I asked him.

"That's Tiger," he replied.

"Tiger?" I questioned.

He ran out of the kitchen and returned shortly with a chubby, red-striped cat named Tiger, hanging over his arms. The cat squirmed in the boy's arms when she saw me. I gently petted her head, but it was too much for her. Tiger wriggled free and darted under the kitchen cupboard. I was relieved Boy was still outside as I wasn't sure how he would react to cats.

I swallowed the last drop of my coffee and stood up.

"I'm going to pack my tent," I announced. "Today I'm hoping to hitchhike to Victoria."

"Good luck," said the woman.

"Can I come with you to Victoria?" the little boy begged.

I laughed. "No, you better stay here with Tiger, alright?"

He looked at me, disappointed, and crawled behind his mother's skirt.

"We went to Victoria a couple of weeks ago," clarified his mother, "and he liked it very much. But now, little man, holidays are over and today you may help me with picking strawberries and making jam."

His little face lit up. "Nice," he said, "strawberries!"

His mother laughed. "You can have a bowl after we've picked them." She stroked his hair.

"Thanks so much for breakfast," I said.

"Wait a minute," she said. She took a piece of paper and a pen and wrote down her name and telephone number. "For when you're in the neigbourhood again."

The boy walked outside with me and played with Boy until I had packed everything in my backpack. His mother called him and he ran back to the house. I walked to the road.

"Here," the little boy shouted, "this is for you." I turned around and saw him carefully walking towards me with a container of strawberries in his hands.

"Oh," I said, "how delicious."

His mother stood in the doorway. I held the container in the air and called out, "Delicious, thanks!"

She waved and said something. She was standing too far away for me to hear what she was saying.

The little boy walked with us to the gate. He hugged Boy and skipped back to the house. "See you," he shouted.

I set up at the corner where the gas station was. Boy roamed around in the grass along the road. His fur glistened from the rain. Slowly, the water seeped through my clothes. I shivered. My coat had a musty, humid smell. It was about time I changed and took a bath.

Passing freight and transport trucks threw a shower of fine mud splatters on me, darkening my shoes with road dirt. My toque was soaked, and my hair hung in wet strands along my face. My hands were wet, and my toes were cold. I scolded the cars that drove by and left me standing in the rain. The coffee and humidity started to affect my bladder. I danced from one foot to the other until I couldn't hold it any longer. I pulled my backpack onto my back and hurried to the bathroom at the gas station. Not long after my bathroom break, I was back in the rain, waiting.

Finally, a grey minivan stopped, and a woman in her fifties got out.

"I saw you half an hour ago while driving by on the other side," she said. "Have you been standing here long?"

"An hour," I said, my teeth chattering.

She opened the back door of the van. My backpack and Boy found a spot in the back.

"I just brought my son to the ferry in Nanaimo," she told me, "and I'm on my way home. You can ride with me until then. Hop in. It's warm in the van."

The inside of the windows steamed up from the moisture in my clothes. It took quite some time before my body stopped shaking.

"What are you going to do in Victoria?" the woman asked.

I didn't have a well-defined plan, so I shrugged.

"How long are you going to stay there?" she asked.

"Until winter is over, and then I'll figure it out from there," I answered.

She looked at me, worried, and kept asking questions. "Where are you from? Do you have relatives?"

"Yes, I have relatives, but I don't want to talk about it right now," I said.

She changed the subject and returned to my plans for the future. "You can't just live in Victoria without having a goal. You can't just hope to get your feet on the ground without knowing what direction you're going," she insisted.

She was right, and it really got me thinking.

"Yes," I hesitated, "that's true. I need some time to think about it."

"Do you have a hobby or something you like to do?" she asked.

She was very nosy, but I was okay answering this question.

"I write stories," I told her. "Maybe I can do something with that. I'm writing a travelogue."

"Oh, nice," she said surprised. "Promise to let me read it when you're done, okay?"

I smiled. "Okay, I promise."

A little later we stopped at the farmers market in Westholme. "Let me know if I can be of some help to you," she said, handing me her business card.

I was building a nice collection. She made me promise again to contact her. My circle of friends on the island was growing.

16. Destination or starting point?

I had almost reached my travel destination and now, after my conversation with the woman, a plan started to form in my head. My list of resolutions for my new life was gradually growing longer: make the right decisions, connect with the right people, give others a second chance, avoid making decisions when tired, and focus on my goals. I was going to get busy realizing those goals.

I positioned myself at a spot on the highway. Soon, Boy and I caught a ride. At the bus station south of Duncan, we got out of the car. Again, we didn't have to wait long. We were dropped off at the big intersection in Mill Bay.

"Come on, Boy, let's buy a cup of coffee at Tim Horton's."

My hands warming around the hot cup, I walked back to the intersection hoping the next driver willing to give me a ride would take us all the way to Victoria.

Luck was on our side.

"We're heading to Victoria to buy school supplies at the Mayfair shopping mall," said the sisters who picked me up in their big pickup truck. "You can ride with us."

They talked non-stop about the upcoming school year, giggling constantly when the conversation turned to boys. I dozed off on the bench seat in the back. The road wound around the Malahat mountain, and way down on the left, I caught a glimpse of the ocean. I made a mental note to return to this spot on a clear day. The view must be spectacular.

After a half-hour drive, the girls dropped me off at the shopping mall.

"Don't party too hard," they shouted from their open windows as they drove off.

I watched them go, smiling.

I had achieved my first goal. My journey was complete. From now on, everything would be fine. The rest couldn't possibly be too difficult. I would find a job, rent a room, and everything would flow smoothly.

Inside the mall was a large round food court with dozens of tables and chairs. Surrounding the area were small restaurants offering delicious dishes from the aroma of Eastern spices to the scent of Western greasy hamburgers. My mouth watered as I sat at my table.

I took out my tablet and turned it on. I opened some of the food I had brought from home. Boy lay at my feet, resting and drying his fur. He had gotten completely soaked in the back of the pickup truck that brought us here. I gave him some dog food. It wasn't yet lunchtime and the place wasn't busy. I felt relaxed as I observed people shopping. A sense of calm washed over me. Here, in this city, I was determined to build my future. It was big enough to accommodate another resident. I was confident I could find a job in one of the many stores here and finding a place to live wouldn't be a problem either. But first, I intended to enjoy the last days of summer before the students returned to school and the Labour Day festivities ended.

I surfed the Internet a bit to check out upcoming events in the city. I sent Pete a message on Facebook to update him on my whereabouts and how things were going. He didn't respond. He was probably at work. I wondered if his father was feeling better and if Pete would be able to join me by the next weekend.

Returning to writing my story, I filled pages with my recent adventures. As the afternoon waned, I closed my computer.

Grabbing my backpack, I headed outside. It was still drizzling and everything seemed grey. Approaching a shop assistant, I asked, "Do you know how to get downtown?"
She pointed towards the highway. "It leads straight into the city centre," she said.
I thanked her and began walking. The highway transformed into a bustling main street lined with beautifully decorated stores. The windows displayed every luxury imaginable. I admired the historical buildings along the way. Warmly lit restaurants looked inviting, filled with people chatting and enjoying their meals. My stomach grumbled, signaling it was dinnertime.
I dropped my backpack onto a bench, stretching out. Everything ached. I settled beside my backpack and pulled out some food.
"Could you spare some change, please?" I heard a slow voice beside me ask.
Startled, I turned to see a weathered-faced First Nations man. His dark eyes looked at me expectantly. He smiled, revealing brown teeth stumps as if trying to reassure me. It didn't quite have the desired effect.
"No, no," I stammered, moving a little further away from him.
Slowly, he nodded, understanding. Shuffling away, he approached another passer-by who also shook his head and walked on. Guilt crept into my conscience. Should I have given him something? I myself had almost nothing. What would he have done with the money? Buy food or alcohol? I couldn't shake off the feeling that I should have been kinder to him. To soothe myself, I resolved to respond more compassionately next time.
It was time to find a place to sleep for the night. I had read online that you could set up a tent in parks as long as you

packed up before 7 a.m. Dusk was approaching, but the end of the long main street was nowhere in sight. I remembered seeing on the map that there was a large park south of the city bordering the ocean.

Lifting my backpack, I continued walking. Finally, at the last major intersection near the Royal BC Museum, I saw a sign pointing towards Beacon Hill Park. That's where I wanted to go. The straps of my backpack dug into my shoulders, and my hips were sore. My shoes and socks were wet, and I could feel blisters forming on my heels.

I wasn't the only one planning to spend the night in the park. Here and there, tents were already set up. I passed an elderly man pushing a cart filled with all his worldly possessions. He was certainly no tourist.

As I ventured deeper into the park, it became clear that most of the people camping there were homeless. They had no other place to sleep. Was it wise for me to set up my tent in this park?

Considering my options, I realized they were limited. Renting a hotel room would drain my funds quickly. And what about tomorrow night? Another hotel? I would be broke in no time. The only viable option seemed to be spending the night here and assessing the situation.

I walked around the park, struggling to find a suitable spot to pitch my tent. Dusk was settling in and I needed to decide soon. Between the trees, darkness would soon descend...

17. Warrior or Worrier?

"You're new here?" asked a guy I passed for the second time. He sat with his knees pulled up in the doorway of his tent, smoking a cigarette, his hoody pulled over his head.

"Yes," I replied, "Honestly, I'm looking for a spot to set up my tent."

"Well," he said, pointing to the spot beside his tent, "come, stay here."

He must have seen the suspicion in my eyes and shrugged. "Take it or leave it, eh."

He puffed on his cigarette, squinting at me through the cloud of smoke he exhaled. There was something childlike in his posture that made me decide to accept his offer.

"Good," I said, letting my backpack slide off my shoulders.

He introduced himself as Rinc, then stood up and gestured with the cigarette in his fingers, showing me how I should set up my tent. While I set up the tent, Rinc and Boy got acquainted and seemed to get along well.

"What are you going to do tomorrow?" Rinc asked.

"I'm going to explore the city," I replied. "After this weekend, I'll start looking for a job and see if I can rent a room."

"Good luck," said Rinc. "Both won't be easy to come by in Victoria after this weekend."

"No?" I asked, feeling alarmed.

"No," he said. "The tourist season is almost over, and finding a job will be tough. And rooms are outrageously expensive."

A light panic welled up within me.

"But you can always try, of course," he added, trying to encourage me.

I nodded silently, considering his words. "I should probably start job hunting right away tomorrow," I decided aloud.

"No, no," said Rinc, shaking his head. "Let's do something fun tomorrow. I know a public square where you can play Scrabble."

I couldn't help but laugh at his spontaneity. We had only known each other for 15 minutes, and he was already trying to make plans.

"Scrabble sounds fun," I said, "I'm in."

It was getting dark, but I could see the grin on his face by the row of white teeth that showed.

"Would you like to come sit at the neighbour's fire for a bit?" Rinc asked, pointing across the field where a couple of tents stood with a fire burning under a tarp. Interested, I agreed, and we headed over to visit the neighbours.

The five men seated around the fire were no ordinary men. They wore layers of clothes that spoke of their familiarity with rugged outdoor life. Each had an unkempt beard and rough hands. A couple greeted me while the others slouched in their lawn chairs, gazing into the flames. Rinc settled on the ground and I followed suit. Soon, the cold dampness seeped through, and I squatted on my haunches.

We didn't linger long. The conversation was aimless, and when Rinc stood up after his third cigarette, I did the same.

"Aren't you staying?" asked one of the men at the campfire, peering at me from under his cowboy hat. His black hair hung to his shoulders. He took a drag from his cigarette, squinting to keep the smoke out of his eyes.

"It's been a long day," I replied. "I want to go to bed."

"I understand," he said slowly, a sly smile curling around his mouth.

Suddenly, the others perked up, and one of them joked, "Hey, Rinc, can I borrow her sometime?" Laughter followed, albeit hushed.

"Shut up," Rinc retorted over his shoulder as he walked away.

I turned and followed him back towards my tent, Boy walking closely beside me.

Rinc hesitated at the entrance of his tent, turning on his phone for light. "If you get cold," he said, nodding towards his tent.

"Are you kidding me?" I burst out. "What do I look like?"

He grinned. "It was worth a shot." With that, he crawled into his tent.

By the beam of my flashlight, I wriggled into my sleeping bag and directed Boy to his spot under the awning. I hoped he would keep watch.

"See you in the morning!" Rinc called out from his tent.

"Good night," I replied, curling up deep in my sleeping bag, shivering.

"Please, protect me, Lord. I feel lonely and afraid," I whispered in prayer before drifting off to sleep.

Indeed, at 7 a.m., the bylaw officer woke us up. He walked over to the neighbours with the campfire to rouse them as well. I crawled out of my tent and started packing my belongings. Rinc was still asleep. I wondered if I needed to wake him myself when the officer returned and shook Rinc's tent door. A grumpy groan was the response.

"Come out, now!" the officer demanded, unrelenting.

Rinc's tent zipper opened, revealing a rough-looking head under a hoodie. "I'm coming, take it easy," Rinc mumbled.

The officer didn't take offense. "When I come back in five minutes, you better be gone," he warned.

"What will you do if I'm not?" Rinc shot back.

The officer didn't reply. Perhaps Rinc challenged him like this every morning. I stepped aside and fed Boy his breakfast. Activity stirred at the neighbouring campfire. They packed up their things, and one by one, the homeless vacated the park. Some carried only large shopping bags, while others, like the old man from yesterday, pushed carts loaded with possessions. The park emptied, and the streets of Victoria absorbed the homeless one by one.

The bylaw officer moved on, and Rinc grumbled as he packed his belongings, hoisting everything onto his back before walking away.

"Where are you off to?" I ventured to ask.

"I'm heading to breakfast at the shelter," he replied.

That seemed like a good idea to me, so I followed him. As we walked along the main street, he softened a bit.

"Sorry," he said, "I'm grumpy in the mornings."

"Really?" I replied sarcastically.

The shelter was bustling with activity. Later, I learned from Internet research that the shelter served over five hundred thousand meals annually. Even without that information, I was impressed by the dedication of the volunteers who worked diligently to serve nutritious food and maintain a welcoming atmosphere at the tables.

18. Labour Day weekend

Shortly after eight, we left the shelter and returned to the street. Even on this early Friday morning, a festive atmosphere hung over the city. Hotels and shops bustled in preparation for a rush of tourists. The weather had cleared, and the sun shone brightly.

Rinc told me about all the events happening in the city.

"Let's do the Ghostly Walk through downtown and Chinatown," he suggested.

"We might want to skip that," I replied, horrified.

"Okay, I'm fine with anything," Rinc said.

The market around the harbour was delightful. I enjoyed browsing the booths where artists sold their paintings and handmade jewelry. At noon, we grabbed sandwiches and listened to a street concert. A stage hosted short sketches and stand-up comedy that kept the crowd entertained. Shortly after, we headed to the Scrabble square. Tables were set up under umbrellas for the games.

"Let's sit here," Rinc said, choosing a table.

During our game of Scrabble, I learned a lot about Rinc.

"The rule is," Rinc explained, "with every word we lay down, we have to say something about ourselves."

I laughed and agreed to the rule.

"I'll start," he said, spelling out the word 'thirty'. "That's how old I am."

"Get out of here," I scoffed. "I thought you were much younger."

"Nope."

It was my turn to place tiles. I formed the word 'two'.

"I have a brother and a sister," I explained.

Rinc spelled out his name. "My name means *'Warrior'*," he said proudly.

He then placed the word 'rent'. I learned he had lived in a rental place last year.

"It drove me crazy trying to scrape together money, so I decided to live on the streets. I thought it was the solution to my problems until I was woken up every morning by the bylaw officer. That's incredibly irritating. If I ever get the chance, I'll live in a house again," he said.

"That would be coming full circle," I remarked dryly.

"You're right," he admitted. "How can I ever rent a house that takes up my entire welfare check? And what landlord wants a tenant without good references?" he added, sighing.

"You know," I teased, "from now on I'm going to call you *'Worrier'* instead of *'Warrior'*."

The sour face he made indicated he didn't find this amusing. I chuckled.

By late afternoon, we walked back to the shelter. At 5 p.m., a delicious, warm meal was served. I felt guilty accepting food while having money in the bank. None of the shelter volunteers questioned me, and like the other homeless guests, I enjoyed a tasty meal. Nearly every chair in the dining hall was occupied. I began to wonder about the stories that brought these individuals here.

Then, Jaxsen came over to our table. He looked about fifty, with leather bracelets and chains adorning his wrists. Kind brown eyes peered out from a face framed by a grey goatee. Waves of blonde-grey hair peeked from under his hat.

"Is this chair free?" he asked, pulling it out.

"Sure," I nodded. "Feel free to join us."

Jaxsen seemed eager to talk. Suddenly, he said, "You're too young to be a guest here."

I raised my eyebrows. "Why?" I asked.

Ignoring my question, he continued, "I'm going to tell you a story, as a warning. You can decide for yourself what to do with it."

"Okay, go ahead," I said with a shrug.

"My life was good," Jaxsen began. "I grew up in a large family and pulled all the pranks imaginable. I didn't enjoy high school and dropped out. Instead, I landed a good job at my father and uncle's construction company. I married and had children."

Jaxsen paused to take a bite of his cheesecake.

"So far, so good," he continued. "Evenings and weekends were spent drinking beer with friends. Then, one day, someone offered me cocaine. I thought, why not try it once? Big mistake, of course. It's highly addictive, and nothing could stop me from wanting more. My marriage fell apart, and the money from selling our house vanished quickly. I ended up on the streets."

"One day I overdosed and ended up in the hospital. Someone from the shelter visited me and offered help. Now I'm detoxing. I often feel miserable, and in weak moments, I'd like to call my buddies and ask for some stuff. But, so far, I've been coming here when I'm down, and it's still going well. I've tried to get clean before, but this time it will happen," Jaxsen opened up to us. "Never start using, girl," he warned, lifting his pointer finger.

I promised.

"Or are you already using?" he asked, examining me carefully.

"No," I said firmly. "I hope I never will."

I hesitated to say more, but then I continued, "I've got a goal in my life I'm working towards."

"What is your goal?" Jaxsen asked, his interest piqued.
I shared with him my ambitions to find a job and rent a room. He nodded thoughtfully.
"That's a good start," he encouraged. "Did you finish high school?"
I nodded, and he gave my shoulder a reassuring pat. "Good, you'll get there."
It was daunting to discuss my plans with others, but I believed it was important for them to know what I was striving for. Others could hold me accountable and offer support when things didn't go as planned.
I wasn't sure if Jaxsen was the right person for this kind of support. The shelter's visitors seemed focused on their own struggles, and I wondered if they could support each other effectively. That was something I still had to figure out.

Saturday also began with beautiful weather. Once again, we were awakened by the bylaw officer. "Get up, everyone!" his harsh voice echoed.
Rinc grumbled annoyedly from inside his tent, but the zipper remained closed. While I packed my belongings, the officer moved on to the other tents. Boy ate the food I set out for him, and by the time his bowl was empty, I saw the officer returning.
"It's always the same old song here," the officer muttered as he shook Rinc's tent. "Get out now!" he shouted.
With deliberate slowness, the tent zipper finally came down, and Rinc crawled out.
"Get lost, man. Go nag someone else," he growled.
"Rules are rules, I'm just doing my job," came the curt response.
"Nice job you have," Rinc scolded.

The officer's eyes spewed fire, his face reddening. Apparently, Rinc had struck a nerve.

The officer steamed. "Boy," he threatened, "my patience with you is running thin."

"And then?" Rinc provoked.

"Then?" The officer took a step towards Rinc. "Then you'd better find another place to sleep."

Rinc laughed scornfully.

"This is your last chance," the officer warned. "If you don't pack your tent right away, tomorrow morning you'll have to leave this park permanently." He turned and walked away.

Spouting all kinds of four-letter words, Rinc packed his stuff. I pulled my backpack onto my back and waited until Rinc was ready to head out.

The sun climbed above the trees, casting beams of white light onto the dewy grass. Maple leaves, already coloured ochre yellow from the summer drought, glowed warmly in the sun's rays. The city was still fairly sleepy, unaware of the homeless people who were rudely awakened to start their day of doing nothing. They would love to make their day shorter and wake up later.

Rinc and I had breakfast at the shelter. We spent the day wandering downtown. My feet were swollen and cramped in my shoes. My arm and back muscles ached from carrying my heavy backpack. The skin, where my backpack rubbed against me, was chafed raw. I saw no opportunity to leave my backpack behind. Perhaps I could leave it at the shelter, though the volunteers might not want the responsibility of watching it.

Rinc seemed distracted today, lost in his thoughts. I tried to start conversations several times, but they fizzled out each time.

"Is something wrong?" I finally asked.

"I'm looking for Cindy," he said as if that explained everything.

"Cindy?" I prompted.

"Yes, Cindy," he growled suddenly. "I've nothing left to smoke." Beads of sweat glistened on his face.

A light went on in my head. I said nothing but felt sorry for him.

We couldn't find Cindy anywhere and Rinc got more and more irritated. He approached people he seemed to know but no one would sell him anything. Even at dinnertime in the shelter, he couldn't find anyone willing to provide him with drugs. We returned to the park and set up our tents. Rinc remained silent, consumed by his troubles.

That night I woke up several times, frightened. I heard Rinc swearing in his tent. I drifted off again, only to be awakened too early by the bylaw officer.

On Sunday morning, I recalled the day about a week ago when I was in the church in Edmonton. It felt like a century had passed, and even longer since I'd left home. Thinking of home brought a sense of freedom. Surprisingly, I didn't miss my family at all.

Today, I planned to go to the library or Tim Horton's. I hoped Pete would be on Facebook. He would surely want to know how I was doing. I didn't have anything special to tell him yet, but that would change soon. Tomorrow, I would start looking for a job. As long as I had some money in the bank, I could buy food and other essentials. But winter was approaching. I needed to ask Rinc, once his morning temper subsided, if I should take extra precautions for the cold.

After breakfast, I had the opportunity to ask. Rinc was still restless, but a few coffees seemed to calm him down.

"You need to get enough clothing and blankets," he advised. "A rain suit is ideal too. It keeps the cold out, but the downside is, you'll sweat in it. That makes you smell and people won't want you in their stores. You have to avoid that."

Slowly but surely, I was learning the ropes of street life. Rinc raised a valid point; I needed to ensure I looked presentable and clean when I started applying for jobs. My first step would be to take a shower at the shelter and make sure my clothes were fresh.

As I finished my breakfast, I watched the volunteers walking back and forth, offering friendly words to everyone. I approached one of them.

"I would like to do volunteer work, too," I said. "How can I help?"

She shook my hand and introduced herself as Ann.

"Let's ask Paul tomorrow," she said. "He's in charge of the volunteer work. He can also tell you about the opportunities we offer to the people living on the streets," she added.

This was like music to my ears. I walked back to Rinc and Boy. Rinc lay with his head on his arms on the table, and Boy lay with his head on his paws under it.

"Hey, you pair of slackers," I laughed and gave them both a gentle push.

Rinc grumbled, and Boy just rolled his eyes. It wasn't going to be easy to stay focused on my own path with people around me who didn't share the same goals. But with the help of the volunteers at the shelter, I felt confident it could happen. I smiled. Maybe it was the sunshine streaming through the windows, but I had a sense that life was good.

After another cup of coffee, we hit the streets again. Rinc had perked up a bit and knew exactly where to find everything I needed. He showed me the library and the stores where I could apply for jobs. I committed it all to memory. With so many opportunities in town, I was convinced I would find work somewhere.

As the city came to life, the streets filled with brightly dressed tourists. The hum of cars, along with people's chatter and laughter, created a festive atmosphere. We walked down to the harbour and wandered among the market stalls. Boy walked obediently on his leash beside me.

Everything was going smoothly until we ran into Cindy...

19. Cindy

Cindy stood with her back against a tree planted in an opening beside the sidewalk. She was Rinc's age. Her hair hung in blonde dreadlocks down to her shoulders. Her washed-out jeans were ripped crossways at the knees and frayed at the ankles. Her eyes were closed, and she sang, gently rocking to the melody she played on her guitar. Tourists threw coins into her guitar case, jingling against the others.
"She has a permit from the city to play music here," Rinc said proudly. "Hey Cindy!" he called.
Cindy looked up. She stopped playing, put her guitar against the tree, and hugged Rinc.
"Cindy, this is Nadia. Nadia, this is Cindy," Rinc introduced. Cindy glanced sideways at me, pulled Rinc by his shirt a couple of steps aside, and started whispering fiercely to him. She dug up joints from her blouse and gave one to Rinc. He took some bills from his back pocket and paid her. They both lit up a joint and not long after, they sank against the tree on the ground and mumbled all kinds of gibberish to each other.
"You want one, too?" Rinc asked.
"No, thank you," I said. "I'd rather stay healthy."
They both burst out laughing.
"We'll see what you have to say later," Cindy said. "When you don't look so neat anymore."
Again, they laughed. It was time to walk away.
"See you later," I called and pulled Boy with me.
I ambled through the market and sat down on the stairs of the Empress Hotel to listen to street artists share their music. The sun bouncing off the water in the harbour hurt my eyes. The

stairs were full of people talking. Suddenly I felt like a lonely island in the middle of a rolling sea.

I pulled out my tablet, but I couldn't see anything on the screen because of the sunlight. I turned it off, picked up my backpack, and plodded in the direction of Fisherman's Wharf.

I walked along the colourful wharf. Canoes and water taxis sat waiting for somebody to rent them for a trip on the ocean. Whale-watching tour boats dropped people off on the pier. Float homes and restaurants lay docked along the wooden walkways. Most of the buildings were two stories high, painted in happy red, yellow, blue, and green. Day tourists were sitting under umbrellas at picnic tables and patios. How nice it would be to live in one of the float homes along the quay. The wooden paths, which gave access to the homes, were full of nosy tourists.

I wondered what it would be like to hear clomping feet and chattering voices going on your little wharf all day long. And, would the residents of a floating home get seasick when it stormed?

I sat down near the wharf on a bench in the shadow of a tree and pulled out my tablet. I had charged it in the morning at the shelter. I wrote more about my train trip and relived the first days away from home all over again. The world around me faded, and I forgot where I was. Would anybody be sad that I had run away? Maybe my father. After all, he came after me on the Saturday evening I left. That was now more than a week ago. By now, he probably would have let the situation go.

I typed until the battery was dead. I then stood up and went looking for a Tim Horton's where I could recharge the tablet and get an Internet connection. It was time to contact Pete.

I heaved my backpack onto my back and started to walk in the direction of Beacon Hill Park. On my way, I saw a Starbucks and changed my plans. I went inside, bought coffee and a blueberry muffin, found a table close to a power outlet, and charged the tablet. I logged in to Facebook. Pete was online.

"Hi Pete," I wrote in a message. I added the cowboy hat selfies I took on the main street of Banff.

"So, there you are, at last. I thought you had died in an accident," came his response directly.

"Sorry, LOL," I wrote.

"LOL??? That's not something to laugh about," he responded.

"I didn't have a chance to be on Facebook any sooner. How is everything over there?"

"Your sister is mad. She says you saddled her with your mother. Now she has to do all the chores."

I burst out laughing.

"Serves her right; she is as lazy as my mother," I wrote back.

"LOL, how's it going with you? Where are you?"

"I'm in Victoria. Tomorrow I'm going job hunting. At night, I set up my tent in a park, which is doable with this weather. When are you coming?"

"Right now, I can't come. It's not going well with my father. The doctor doesn't know what's wrong with him, but my father feels miserable."

That was a big bummer. First Rinc abandoned me for Cindy and now Pete wasn't able to come. I sighed and stared out of the window at the rushing traffic. So many unfamiliar people in a big, busy city. At this moment, it seemed like I was on my own.

"Let me know when you can come," I wrote.

"Okay," Pete replied, "I've to go." And he was gone.

I could only guess why he left so fast. Did somebody walk into his room? I logged out, drank the last bit of coffee, went to the bathroom, and dragged myself, backpack and all, out the door. Boy had been sleeping outside in the shade and happily wagged his tail when he saw me again. I untied his leash from the lamppost I had attached him to, and together we walked to the park.

Rinc was already at the campsite. He was lying on his backpack with his head hidden in his hood, and was snoring. He hadn't even made the effort to set up his tent. It seemed like he'd had a rough day. I felt sorry for him. Was he really ten years older than me? He looked so boyish.
I spread out a tarp on the ground and put my tent on it. Boy sniffed at Rinc's shoes and looked at him, questioningly. Rinc didn't notice; he was completely out. The sun sank behind the trees. I thought it was better to help Rinc set up his tent before it got completely dark. Cindy was nowhere to be seen. She probably stayed the night in another part of the city.
I softly shook Rinc's shoulder, but it did nothing. He snored like a monster truck. I searched for something to put under his head so I could take away his backpack. Since it wasn't likely to rain, I used the tarp that was supposed to be the awning of my tent. I lifted his head and took away the backpack. A disgusting liquor smell came out of Rinc's half-open mouth. I attempted to hold my breath and shoved the tarp under his head. Rinc mumbled something and turned, but he kept sleeping.
I searched in his backpack and pulled out his tent. A set of small camping pots came with it and fell clanking on the ground. Suddenly, Rinc shot up.
"Dirty thieves," he screamed, "stay away from my stuff!"
He stood up and came threateningly towards me.

"What are you doing?" he screamed again.

A couple of heads poked out from the other tents a little further away. Somebody walked towards us.

"I wanted to set up your tent," I said defensively. I took a couple of steps backward and held my hands up protectively. Boy started to growl.

The man who was now near enough to hear everything said, "Calm down, Rinc, nothing is going on."

I recognized the voice and saw it was Jaxen, whom we met in the shelter. He firmly grabbed Rinc by his upper arms and tried to calm him down. Rinc kept lashing out, saying that everybody had to leave his stuff alone and that nobody could be trusted.

"Stop now," Jaxen finally said with a resolute voice. "Nadia isn't going to steal from you; she's your friend."

"Friend," Rinc sneered. "She's not. I've only known her a couple of days; maybe she's a spy from the government."

A smile appeared on Jaxen's face. "That's enough now," he said. "Set up your tent and go back to sleep."

I thanked Jaxen and sat down in my tent, my door zipper open. Boy lay down at the entrance. I tried to write some more, but the light of the tablet was too bright for my eyes now that it was getting dark outside. I closed it and lay down in my sleeping bag with my head towards the door so I could see what Rinc was up to. I didn't trust him anymore. So that's how he behaved when he had been drinking and using drugs. Rinc attempted to set up his tent but struggled. He stood there, complaining and swearing. I stepped out of my tent, grabbed the stuff, and helped him. In no time the tent was set up. Rinc disappeared into his tent without a 'thank you'.

I'd see how things go tomorrow. Maybe the air would be cleared by then. If not, I would look for another camping spot tomorrow night. I had no intention of letting my life be ruled again by someone else, especially somebody else's mood. I'd had enough of that.

That night, I slept restlessly. Rinc snored loudly, and Boy growled once. While it was fairly quiet at the other tents, they kept talking late into the evening around the campfire.

20. Job hunting

The next morning, I crawled out of my tent before the bylaw officer came by. Labour Day weekend was over, and I couldn't wait to start job hunting. At 8 a.m., the showers opened at the shelter. I wanted to be one of the first there to wash all the street dirt off of me.
I threw dog kibble into Boy's bowl, and after he finished, I poured water into it. He drank it all and rubbed his wet nose against my hands to show his gratitude. I grabbed his head and playfully dragged him back and forth. He broke loose and barked. Not wanting any noise so early in the morning, I grabbed him again and gave him a firm hug. He wiggled loose, danced around me, and barked even louder in pure excitement.
Rinc woke up. The door of his tent opened, and his messy head appeared. He grumbled something.
"Good morning to you, too," I answered.
He crawled out and crouched on his haunches in front of his tent. He held his head with his hands and moaned.
"Sorry for last night," he muttered.
I was torn between accepting his apology and not bringing up the issue again or admonishing him. From experience with my mother, brother, and sister, I knew that if I didn't address it, his behavior might escalate.
"Are you always so nasty when you're drunk?" I asked.
"No," he growled. "I did it because you touched my stuff, not because I was drunk."
"Yeah, right," I said suspiciously. "Suddenly you didn't know me anymore."

"I knew exactly who you were," he grumbled, "but if you touch my stuff and steal it, I'd have nothing anymore. I'd have to start all over again."

"But I told you that I wanted to help you set up your tent," I insisted.

"Why would I believe that?" he sneered. "Who does that, setting up a tent for somebody else? Why would you do that?"

"What?" I exclaimed. "You don't believe there are people who want to help you? Open your eyes, man. Look at the volunteers at the shelter. Look at the other homeless that live around you. Everybody helps each other."

"It only looks that way," he snarled. "If you knew them better, you would know they steal from each other."

I was still for a moment. Was he right? I didn't know much about these people yet.

I shrugged. "Maybe what you're saying is true," I admitted, "but there are people everywhere, in every group, that help each other, and yes, there are always rotten apples in those groups."

"I'm glad you get it," Rinc said tiredly.

It was time to go to the shelter.

"Are you coming?" I asked.

Rinc pulled himself up with difficulty and packed his stuff. Packed and ready, we dragged ourselves along the main street in the direction of the shelter. After breakfast, I took a shower. I felt wonderfully refreshed standing in front of the mirror while brushing my hair. I left my hat off, so my hair could dry. In good spirits, I walked back to the dining hall.

Rinc was sitting at a table with two older men and I pulled up a chair.

"So, so," the old man beside me said, you're a redhead," and he laughed, showing the few teeth he had left in his mouth.

Oh no, not that again, I thought, always this teasing about my red hair.

The man examined my face and hair as if he never had seen anything like that before. "You're a very beautiful girl," he said sincerely.

I stared at him in disbelief. Rinc and the other man suddenly stopped their conversation and observed us with interest. I felt shy; a warm blush crept up from my neck to my face.

"He's right," Rinc affirmed, and the other man nodded enthusiastically.

"Oh, well," I said, attempting to deflect their comments, but it didn't work.

"You have such beautiful blue eyes," the old man continued. The other man chimed in, "I like your freckles."

Meanwhile, Rinc was scrutinizing me from head to toe. I shifted uncomfortably in my chair and pulled Boy closer to me by his leash.

Rinc noticed. "We're allowed to be honest, right?" he asked.

"Okay," I said, smiling shyly. Drops of sweat trickled down through my just-washed hair onto my neck. I didn't know accepting compliments would be such hard work.

When my hair was dry and I saw the opportunity, I stood up to leave.

"Leave your backpack here," Ann said after I told her I was going to apply for jobs.

"I'll keep an eye on it."

"Boy, you stay with me today," said Rinc, petting the dog on his head. Boy didn't agree. He followed me to the door and ignored Rinc when he called him back. The screaming episode from the night before was probably still in his head.

"Sorry, Rinc." I shrugged apologetically and put Boy on his leash. I would have to tie him up outside the stores to avoid him being taken by the police or wandering off by himself.

I slowly walked down the main street and looked in the shop windows. I decided to go inside a music store. At that moment, there were no customers and nobody was behind the counter. The store felt like an oasis of rest. Soft background music came from the speakers. Beautiful shiny guitars, saxophones, and trumpets were displayed on the shelves. In the middle of the space was a piano waiting invitingly for somebody to sit on the bench and play. In the back of the store was an array of percussion instruments. I sure would like to work there.

From behind an enormous drum, a voice sounded. "I'm coming. Just a minute, please."

A little later, a man appeared from behind the instruments. "How can I help you, young lady?" he asked. He was short, balding, and had a friendly face.

"I'm looking for a job," I said.

A serious frown appeared on his face.

"Unfortunately, I can't help you with that," he said, contemplating. "The busy season has just ended. Our next busy time will not be until December when we'll see an increase in customers again."

"That's too bad," I said. "Thanks for your time."

I turned around and walked to the door. The man's gaze prickled on my back. With my hand on the doorknob, I turned and gave him a nod. Man, I thought, annoyed, stop staring and go back to your percussion instruments.

Hesitantly, the man turned around.

I closed the store door behind me, took in a deep breath, and walked further down the main street. I visited an antique store, then a candy store, clothing store, toy store, thrift store, book store, pharmacy, and a bowling alley, but everywhere I heard the same old song, 'Sorry, the tourist season is over; come back closer to Christmas.' At the big chain stores, I filled out application forms. The shelter was my postal address. Ann had told me I was allowed to do that.

Close to the end of the afternoon, I still hadn't achieved any results. I decided to go to McDonald's. I had an aversion to serving unhealthy food, but maybe I could start there and then look further. Believe it or not, I got hired! McDonald's desperately needed people. The holidays were over, and the young workers who had been there during the summer had gone back to school. With mixed feelings, I filled out the paperwork. I could start half-days, part-time. I had to show up the next morning at eight.

Quite discouraged, I walked back to the shelter. Half-day shifts were not enough to rent a room for myself. I had to find another way to bring in some extra income.

At the shelter, I saw Jaxsen sitting at a table, and I joined him. I wanted to tell somebody my story.

"Hi Jaxsen, tomorrow I start a job at McDonald's," I said, getting straight to the point.

"Good for you," Jaxsen said slowly.

Whenever somebody said to me 'Good for you', a feeling would creep over me like they didn't mean it. A feeling that the other person was somewhat jealous, or thought I was stupid, or just wasn't interested in what they just heard.

Jaxsen seemed lost in his thoughts, but after a couple of moments he mumbled, "They sell junk there. If you eat that garbage every day, you're going to look like Round Hank," and he nodded toward a table a little further away. A man was sitting there who needed at least two chairs to sit properly. His belly hung over his knees, and he had a double chin that almost reached his chest. I stared with wide-open eyes at the man.

"Wow," I said slowly.

"Lack of motivation and money, food addiction, and who knows what other problems he has," explained Jaxsen, as if he had read my judgmental thoughts.

I felt ashamed of the disgust that must have been written all over my face. Jaxsen would surely assume I was judging him too. If I judged somebody who took such poor care of himself as Round Hank, then I would probably also judge somebody addicted to drugs or alcohol.

To save face, I said, "Can the volunteers from the shelter help him?"

Jaxsen looked at me as if he didn't trust the change in my attitude. Then he said, "He has to want it, otherwise it will not work."

I nodded. "I understand."

I let the subject rest. The topic was too sensitive to discuss with Jaxsen, who was trying to climb out of the pit of drug addiction.

I stood up and approached Ann.

"Is it possible to talk to Paul?" I asked.

"Come with me," she said, leading me to Paul's office. His desk was covered in papers, and he was on the phone.

"Have a seat," Ann instructed and turned to leave. "I've got to get back to work, but ask him what you need to ask."

It didn't take long for Paul to finish his call.

"I would like to volunteer here," I said after introducing myself. "I've got a part-time job in Victoria and I would like to spend my off-hours helping here."

"Good," he said. "First, let me tell you something about the work we do here."

Paul talked about the people who come to the shelter and the meals they can receive. He gave me a tour of the building, showing me the spotless shower stalls where people could clean up. We walked through rooms where help was offered to people seeking jobs. The painting and writing rooms especially caught my attention. Students from the local college taught computer courses, and a lady was leading a choir.

Paul mentioned doctors, therapists, vets, and dentists who offered their services for free, which were gratefully accepted by the homeless. And if that wasn't enough, he told me about the people living on the second floor of the building who were being helped to integrate into society and improve their lives.

At the end of the tour, my head was spinning.

I expressed interest in the painting and writing courses, and Paul promised to introduce me to the teacher.

With a head full of expectations, I returned to the breakfast room. I had made my first valuable contacts for a new beginning.

21. McDonald's

I walked to work the next morning, feeling encouraged. Selling Big Macs wasn't the dream job I had hoped for, but nevertheless, I was determined to do my best. On my afternoons off, I planned to visit other businesses to find extra work.

I was greeted by the restaurant manager with a casual, "What was your name again?" Without waiting for my answer, he ordered me to follow him. With short, brisk steps, he led me to the employees' room. He wore a short-sleeved shirt and a diagonally striped tie, his black hair stiff with gel. He handed me my uniform from a rack and pushed it into my hands.

"Go change in the washroom. I'll see you shortly."

I put on my new clothes and thought I looked quite nice in the black and grey uniform. I threaded my red ponytail through the hole in the back of my black cap. Fortunately, they didn't have red uniforms here; that wouldn't have gone well with my freckles.

"Come," said the manager as soon as I returned to the employees' room. "I'll introduce you to Sandra. She'll train you today."

Sandra was a pale, skinny girl.

"Hi," she said in a lackluster tone.

Together, we worked on the frontline at the till.

There was an enormous lineup of people waiting for their egg and sausage McMuffins. The smell of frying eggs and bacon on the hot plates made the restaurant deliciously aromatic, though I didn't have much time to enjoy it. Sandra took the orders, and I ran back and forth to deliver the food and drinks to the right people. Soon, I could guess which customers would choose which meals. The Round Hanks in the lineup weren't the ones buying yogurt and fruit.

After the breakfast rush, groups of retired men came in for coffee and socializing. Young mothers with toddlers took a break from shopping. As lunchtime approached, the lineup at the till grew again, and chicken sandwiches, fries, and salads flew off the counter like hotcakes.

At 1 p.m., at the end of my shift, my head spun from remembering so many product variations and facing so many different people. I sighed with relief the moment I stepped into the sunlight. Boy was exuberantly happy to see me. He had spent the whole morning in a well-shaded spot. I smelled like grease and was eager to wash myself clean as soon as possible. We went to the shelter, where I took a hot shower and scrubbed the cooking smells from my body with the fruit-scented shampoo that was in the shower stall.

Half an hour later, refreshed, I walked through the streets again.

As soon as daylight broke the next morning, I crawled out of my sleeping bag and prepared myself for work. I knew arriving late wasn't acceptable, a point the manager had made clear yesterday. 'You go find a job somewhere else,' he had told a coworker who was late.

I packed up my tent and sleeping bag and headed to the restaurant. As soon as I entered, the manager approached me. "I find it courageous to be homeless and have a job, trying to keep both feet on the ground," he began, "but do you really have to drag that backpack with you? From now on, leave it at the shelter or wherever you stay. Understood? Tomorrow, no backpack in the lunchroom," he emphasized. "The rest of the workers need some space too. Imagine if everyone brought all their belongings here."

His stern gaze conveyed that he meant business. I nodded, resolving to go job hunting again that afternoon.

In the afternoon, I visited five stores inquiring about job opportunities, but to no avail. Disheartened, I went to the library. I checked to see if Pete was on Facebook, but he seemed to still be at work. I tried working on my story for an hour, but my thoughts were scattered by the recent changes in my life.

I rested my elbows on the table, my chin in my hands, staring at the screen. My life so far felt like a disaster. Alone, with a part-time job that barely covered expenses, living in a tent as winter approached. While Victoria had Canada's mildest winter climate, it could still freeze and snow and the thought of enduring the cold and wetness of a temperate rainforest weighed on me.

At dinner in the shelter, I spoke with Ann. "My manager said I can't bring my backpack to work anymore. What should I do?"

"We'll figure something out," Ann reassured me, arranging a spot in the shelter where I could store my backpack. "Do you know anyone who might be able to dogsit Boy?" I asked. "I'm worried my boss won't be happy if he sees Boy tied to a tree all morning."

"Amy might be able to help," Ann suggested, pointing to an elderly woman at a table by the window with two dogs at her feet.

22. Poor Amy

I took my plate and walked towards Amy.
"Is this chair free?" I asked her.
"Go ahead," she said. I noticed she only had one front tooth. Her thin, grey hair hung in strands along her hollow face.
Boy had walked over with me, and the three dogs sniffed each other. Amy petted Boy's head. The dogs seemed to get along well.
"What are the names of your dogs?" I asked Amy.
"Tristan and Isolde," she said. She pulled them one by one towards her and petted their thick, curly, light brown fur with her bony hands. "They're Goldendoodles, a cross between a Golden Retriever and a Poodle."
"What nice dogs," I said admiringly. "There must be a reason why you called them Tristan and Isolde."
Amy nodded. "Do you know the story of Tristan and Isolde?"
I thought for a moment. "I'm not sure anymore how the story went," I said hesitantly.
Amy sat up a bit straighter in her chair. She put the last strings of spaghetti on her fork with her thumb and put it in her mouth. While she was chewing, she looked at me with squinted eyes. Did she want to gauge if I was worth telling the whole story to? Then she started.
"Back in the days when I was still in high school, I always looked forward to the English literature lessons. When the teacher was reading to us, I would sit on the edge of my seat. The story of Tristan and Isolde touched a special place inside me. The story plays out during the reign of King Arthur, you know, that one with the Knights of the Round Table. Isolde

was the daughter of the king of Ireland. She was given in marriage to King Mark of Cornwall. King Mark sent his cousin Tristan to Ireland to escort Isolde to Cornwall. Dumb move by the king. During the journey, Isolde and Tristan fell in love with each other. Isolde married Mark of Cornwall, but this couldn't change the fact that she still loved Tristan. The bond between the two remained after the marriage.

When King Mark finally found out, he forgave Isolde, but Tristan got banned from Cornwall. Tristan left for Brittany in France. There he met Iseult. He felt attracted to her because her name was similar to his true love's name. He married her but didn't sleep with her because he only had love for the 'true' Isolde. When he fell ill, he sent a ship to pick up Isolde in the hope she would cure him. If she was coming, the sails of the returning ship would be white; if not black. Iseult, who saw the white sails of the ship, lied to Tristan and told him the sails were black. He died of grief before Isolde could reach him. Isolde died soon after of a broken heart."

For a moment, Amy was quiet and sank deep into thought. She then continued her story.

"At that time, I was in love with a boy in my class. My father didn't allow me to date before I was 18, and I told the boy so. He said he was crazy about me, but he passed me by for another girl in my class whose parents allowed her to date. I still remember the pain of being so easily exchanged for somebody else. It wasn't until two years later, after our final exam, we all left school. We went our separate ways and I never saw any of them again. I never forgot the burning, stinging feeling in my heart. I understood how it was possible to die from a broken heart."

"But why did you name your dogs Tristan and Isolde?" I asked. "Now it constantly reminds you of your pain."

"I did that," she said, "to never forget that I'm not the only one that doesn't get what she hoped for. It prevents me from drowning in self-pity."

She wiped her eyes with a corner of her sleeve.

"Later on," she continued, "I married a sweet man who wasn't very smart with money. I didn't know that until he died and left me with an enormous debt. He always said that I didn't have to work and that he would look after us. That was sweet of him, but also a bit dumb. Now I can't do anything; I've no work experience, and nobody will hire me." A tear slid down her ashen cheek. With a trembling, lamenting voice, she continued, "As long it's summer, everything is okay with me. But as soon as winter begins and the sun disappears, when it rains every day and the days shorten, I become so terribly sad. I can't get up in the morning, and I cry the whole day. I wouldn't be able to go to work. The days are already starting to shorten, and the fear is starting to paralyze me. It's horrible that the bylaw officer comes to kick everybody out of their tents. It's just awful. I don't want to think about it, about tomorrow morning, I mean, if you understand what I mean."

She rubbed her wrinkled cheeks to wipe away her tears. Black stripes of dirt stayed behind. I nodded feeling my eyes stinging.

I hesitated about asking her to dogsit Boy while I was working, but I went ahead and to my surprise, Amy's face lit up.

"I would love to do that. It would give me a reason to get out of my sleeping bag in the morning," she said. "Where are you going to work?"

"At McDonald's," I said apologetically.

Amy didn't seem to have any prejudice against the fast-food chain. On the contrary, she asked, "Can you bring me something to eat as a favour in return?"

I assured her I could make that happen and promised her.

Amy's tent wasn't far from my camping spot, and we agreed that I would bring Boy to her in the morning.

I twirled a couple of strands of spaghetti around my fork and put it in my mouth. The food had grown cold, but that didn't bother me. I was happy with the agreement we had made.

A couple of days later, I started to doubt if I still liked the arrangement. Early in the afternoon, I walked from the restaurant to the park. It was mild and sunny September weather. Lunchtime was almost over, and office workers took the opportunity to do some small grocery shopping or get food.

On a street corner, I saw Amy with the three dogs. People stood around them in a half-circle. What was going on over there? I started walking quickly. Amy wasn't in trouble, was she?

As I came closer and stood on my toes to look over the heads of the bystanders, I saw that Amy had the dogs performing tricks. She had spread two small blankets on the sidewalk, and Tristan and Isolde each lay down on one. The dogs picked up a corner of their blanket and rolled themselves in it. The people clapped and laughed. Boy stood there looking somewhat sheepish. He held a cap in his mouth, and the people threw coins into it.

How clever, I thought.

Amy took a ball from her bag, and her two dogs sat on their hind legs in front of her. Amy threw the ball to Tristan, and he caught it in his front paws. She repeated the trick with Isolde, who also caught the ball perfectly.

Then Boy spotted me standing in the audience, and his tail started wagging. He walked towards me with the cap still in his mouth. I noticed Amy looking up, visibly concerned.

"Boy, come here," she called out.

I waved at Amy and smiled. Taking the cap from Boy, I brought it over to Amy. She grabbed the cap with both hands, a flash of suspicious fear crossing her eyes as she looked at me.

To break the tension, I said casually, "What nice tricks you have taught the dogs. It looks like you have a job too. You have your own dog theater."

She smiled, revealing her single tooth, and petted her dogs on their heads.

"I'm very proud of them," she said.

"Do you make any money with it?" I asked.

"For sure," she replied, "I'm even saving some money. There's a young man in the park who manages my money."

My stomach tightened. What kind of person played banker in a park where homeless people lived?

"Who is that remarkable person?" I asked cautiously.

"Jayden," she said.

"Jayden," I repeated slowly. "He sounds like an interesting guy. I'd like to meet him."

"That's great," said Amy, "I'll introduce you to him." She packed her belongings into her shopping cart, and we started walking toward the park.

"Sometimes," Amy continued, "I don't have much to deposit. Sometimes I need a couple of cognacs, and that costs money. The summers are good for savings. Jayden writes down everything I give him, so I know exactly how much I've saved so far."

What a polite gentleman, I thought sarcastically. I could hardly wait to meet him.

We shuffled towards the park. Amy pushed her rambling shopping cart ahead of her. I noticed people glancing at us, and I pulled my toque deeper over my head. Was I ashamed to be seen walking with Amy? I was as homeless as she was. Did I not want to be associated with homeless people? Were there gradations in homelessness, a hierarchy even? What was the actual reason I was ashamed? Was it because I felt superior? Was I afraid to meet somebody from work, risking my job? I should be ashamed for thinking I was better than Amy. Above all, I should be ashamed for hesitating to be seen with a homeless person, while benefiting from the shelter's help.

I was relieved as we left the bustling main street behind us. The park felt pleasantly peaceful.

23. Banker Jayden

We found Jayden in the park, slumped on a bench. Smoke curled upwards from under the black hoodie pulled over his head.

"Hi Jayden," Amy greeted, "this is Nadia. Nadia, this is Jayden."

"Hi," I said.

Jayden looked at me with glazed eyes from a pale face. His pupils were dilated, likely from the drugs he was using.

"I told Nadia that you manage my money," said Amy.

"Hmmm," Jayden mumbled.

"You write everything on a list, right?" she asked.

"Hmmm," he responded again.

"Maybe you can manage Nadia's money too," Amy suggested.

"Amy," I began, alarmed. I touched her arm but pulled back my hand immediately, curious about Jayden's reaction. That quickly became clear. Jayden put his legs under the bench and pulled himself up, a flicker of interest in his eyes.

"I can arrange that for you," he said.

"What are the terms and conditions?" I asked cautiously.

"Terms and conditions?" Jayden echoed. "What do you mean?"

"Can I withdraw money when I need something extra?"

"Yes, hello!" he said, "I'm not a bank."

"Okay," I said. "I understand that. What happens when I've saved a lot and want to, for example, buy a house or a car? Can I withdraw it then?"

Jayden sat up even straighter, his eyes growing more intense.

"Do you make a lot of money or something?" he asked nonchalantly, exhaling a cloud of smoke.

I nodded, picturing myself at McDonald's, shuttling orders from the kitchen window to the waiting customers.

Jayden rummaged in his inside pocket and pulled out a crumpled little notebook. From another pocket, he retrieved a pen.

"How much would you like to deposit today?" he asked.

"Oh," I said hastily, "I'm still exploring all my options. I want to know what gives me the most benefits. Maybe I'll go to a regular bank, or perhaps there's someone else in the park who can manage my money for me."

"Hmm," Jayden said suspiciously, leaning his elbows on his knees. He peered at me from under his hoodie, as if trying to gauge how he could convince me to entrust my money to him.

"Or," he suggested, "you could use my services."

"He's very good with finances, eh," Amy interrupted.

I nodded at her.

"Show me," I said to Jayden. "How would you write it down when I bring you something? Maybe you can show me Amy's list as an example," I added carefully.

Jayden placed his cigarette in his mouth to free his hands, then flipped through the pages of the notebook, revealing several lists. Are there really that many people who give their money to a drug addict to manage it for them? I wondered silently.

"Look," Jayden said, displaying Amy's page. I saw a list with numbers that, when added up, amounted to a few hundred dollars. Likely, it had all gone up in smoke, literally.

Again, I nodded. "I've got to think about it," I said, "I'll let you know when I've made a decision."

Jayden slumped back on the bench, visibly tired. He pulled his hoodie further over his head, retreating into his own world.

"Come," Amy said, breaking the silence. "Let's go. Jayden has more things to do."

I remained silent, taken aback by Amy's naivety.

That evening, after dinner in the shelter, I approached a volunteer and explained the situation. I asked if he would speak to Amy, encouraging her to deposit her money elsewhere.

The volunteer shook his head. "I'm sorry," he said. "We'd like to help, but Amy is convinced that Jayden is a good man. Sooner or later, she'll realize her money is gone.

As it turned out, that realization came sooner than I expected.

The week that followed brought rain every day. Grey skies blanketed the city, soaking my clothes and sleeping bag with persistent dampness. I had no dry threads left on my body, and the clothes reeked from the moisture.

"Don't you have deodorant or something?" Sandra, my morning coworker, wrinkled her nose in distaste.

"Sorry, I forgot this morning," I lied.

That afternoon, I headed straight to the laundromat to toss my dirty clothes into a washing machine.

The rainy, sombre weather took its toll on Amy as well. She trudged through the streets of Victoria with Tristan and Isolde trailing behind her, pushing her grocery cart ahead. The neck of a cognac bottle protruded from between plastic bags containing her belongings. Occasionally, she paused under store awnings, casting furtive glances around to see if anyone might report her to the police, taking a swig from the bottle.

"Cognac keeps me going," she told me.
I looked at her questioningly. I didn't say anything, but I feared her legs might give out if she took another drink.
"I only have twenty dollars left in my pocket," Amy complained. "That's only enough to buy one bottle of cheap liquor. And I can't make money in this weather. Are you coming with me to ask Jayden for some of my money?"
I hesitated, unsure whether to advise her against it or to simply accompany her. I opted for the latter. Amy needed support for what she was about to do, and her reluctance to go alone indicated her uncertainty about her 'bank'.
Together, we walked to the park. Jayden sat on his bench, completely soaked and seemingly unfazed by the weather. Smoke curled from under his hoodie. In the distance, other homeless individuals were already setting up tents on the grass.
"Hi Jayden," Amy opened the conversation. "What terrible weather, eh? Don't you think?"
Jayden responded with his usual noncommittal "hmm."
"All this grey makes me miserable," Amy continued.
Jayden nodded slightly but remained slouched in his seat.
"I need something to cheer me up," Amy continued, "a little cognac would do wonders."
"Hm-mm," Jayden anwered again.
Amy wiped the wet strands of hair from her face and tried to sniff away a drop hanging from her nose. When that didn't work she wiped it on the sleeve of her dirty coat.
"I only have twenty dollars left," she continued bravely. "I want to withdraw some money." She smoothed her skirts and adjusted her shawl, looking expectantly at Jayden.
"That's not possible today," Jayden said bluntly. He slid further down on the bench, stretching out his legs. Amy and I took a step backward.

Amy looked desperately from Jayden to me and back. She burst out, "But I really need it. Look at the weather. It's unbearable without cognac."

Jayden lost his patience. He jumped up. "Woman," he yelled. "You yourself said you still have twenty dollars left. That's plenty for today." Realizing he had gone too far, he softened his tone, "Come back tomorrow. Then you can get your money." He dropped back onto the bench.

Amy too had reached her breaking point. She screamed, "It's my money! Keep your paws off it!" She raised her fist and stepped towards Jayden. But what could an old woman like her possibly do against such a young man? Jayden stood up. Before Amy's fist could reach him, Jayden knocked her to the ground.

"Amy!" I heard myself screaming. Bewildered, I dropped my heavy backpack, rushed to Amy, and knelt beside her. Her nose was bleeding, and her whole body trembled. Meanwhile, Tristan and Isolde barked wildly, jumping against Jayden's legs.

People emerged from their tents, running towards us.

"What's going on?" asked a bearded homeless man, grabbing Jayden by the sleeve.

"They robbed me earlier today, and now I can't give Amy any money," Jayden explained, yanking his sleeve loose.

"Who robbed you?" Beard Man asked, scanning the area.

Jayden's seemingly innocent remark, "somebody who lives close by," unwittingly ignited a cascade of conflict among the homeless group gathered around him. His gesture pointed toward the group itself, caused confusion.

"Was that you?" somebody asked the person beside him.

"What?" he said upset. "You probably mean yourself," and he gave the person asking the question a push.

The initial push in response to the accusation set off a chain reaction of accusations flying back and forth. Each member of the group, already burdened with their own struggles and resentments, found an outlet for their frustrations in this sudden confrontation. What began as a misunderstanding quickly escalated into a full-blown fight, with punches thrown and voices raised in fury.

The bylaw officer came jogging over. "What's going on here?" he barked.

Meanwhile, Amy stood up, still trembling all over. I pulled her away a little from the fight.

"Jayden started this. He stole my money," she explained to the officer, her voice quivering.

"Who's Jayden?" he asked, searching the group.

During the commotion, Jayden had secretly disappeared. The swearing and threats that followed were now directed at Jayden. "We'll teach him a lesson when we see him," the group threatened in unity.

The bylaw officer pushed the group apart. "Back to your tents, everybody," he commanded. "I want quiet in the park or I'll kick you all out!"

Grumbling, everybody dispersed to their camping spot. Still numbed by the screaming and the fight, Amy and I also walked away.

We didn't see Jayden for the next couple of days, and it seemed Amy had forgotten about the incident. It didn't sit well with me.

"Have you heard anything about Jayden?" I asked her one evening, as we both sat in the door openings of our tents, waiting for dusk.

"No, I haven't seen him yet," she said.

"Too bad about your money," I continued, "and about the other people's money he played banker for."
"Oh, yes," she said stoically, "that was the risk I was taking. He probably needed the money."
"Yeah, hello!" I said angrily, "he used it for drugs."
"Well," said Amy, "just as I said, he probably needed it." She pulled a blanket over her head and sank into her misery.
Infuriated, I crawled into my sleeping bag and zipped the tent door shut. I finally calmed down when Rinc stood at my door and asked if I wanted to come to the neighbour's fire and talk a bit.
Together we walked through the darkened park, Boy following us. I was glad Rinc and Boy were with me; I wouldn't sit with those guys by myself.
Just like last time, there were beercans strewn under each camp chair. Cowboy Hat was there as well. The chair beside him was empty.
"Do you want to sit here?" he pointed.
I sat down after first moving the chair away from him a little. His eyes shamelessly wandered over my body. I looked away from him. It hadn't been such a good idea to come here.
"Have you found your way a bit now?" he asked, leaning closer. I grabbed the armrests of the chair with both hands and moved further away from him.
He grinned. "You're not afraid of me, right, girlie?"
"No," I said as casually as possible, "I like to have some space."
His black eyes mocked me, telling me he didn't believe me.
"I found a job," I told him. "Hopefully, I won't have to camp out in the park for much longer."
"Too bad," he said. "I like having such special company."

I glanced at him sideways. Did I imagine it, or did he just glide his tongue over his lips? In any case, that obscure little smile played around the corners of his mouth again.

After ten uncomfortable minutes, I stood up.

"I'm leaving," I announced.

Cowboy Hat stood up, too, towering high above me. "I'll bring you to your tent," he said.

"That's not necessary," I said hastily.

Rinc looked at me and also stood up. "I'm leaving. Nadia can walk with me."

Something flared up in Cowboy Hat's black eyes, but he didn't say anything. He didn't make an effort to step aside when I walked out of the circle. My shoulder touched his broad chest. He leaned over and whispered in my ear, "Goodbye, girlie. Till next time."

A shivering ran down my back, and I dared not turn around until I reached my tent. Cowboy Hat remained in his chair, which he had turned slightly to face our tents.

That night, Boy slept in my tent, and my prayer to God was urgent, "Lord, please keep watch over me tonight."

The next morning, I fed the three dogs with the dog food I had bought for Boy as Amy kept forgetting to feed her own dogs.

24. Thanksgiving

One of the goals I kept working on was to find an extra job. My manager shook his head at the end of every week when I asked for more hours. Although I searched everywhere for additional work, my efforts weren't rewarded.

I started to doubt myself. Was it my appearance that worked against me? Did I really look so ugly with my red hair and freckles? Sometimes I thought back to the compliments the men in the shelter had given me. I didn't think the compliments had much worth anymore. It made sense they had said that, I reasoned. They looked so shoddy and neglected that anything that looked a bit cleaner than them was beautiful in their eyes. Their opinions were therefore of no value or was it because I gave the shelter as my address that I couldn't find any extra work?

Whatever the reason, it didn't stop my heart from sinking to the bottom of my shoes whenever I thought about the winter. It was already chilly to sleep outside, although the label inside my sleeping bag said it should keep me warm to ten degrees below zero.

Even though Victoria, with the warm ocean surrounding the city, was the most ideal place on the island for sleeping outdoors, I wasn't the only one not looking forward to the winter. Apart from Amy, who became miserable from lack of sunlight and too much rain, others became aggressive when talking about winter.

"We have the right to affordable housing!" Natasha screamed during dinner one night in the shelter. She stood in the middle of the dining hall with her fist above her head. Others agreed with her. Natasha didn't look like a homeless person. She had long, dark, curly hair that shone under the lights. Her face had a healthy colour. Even her jeans and her hoodie looked clean.

"It's not enough that we are allowed to stay in the parks at night, but have to move on in the morning," she shouted again. "We can't mentally deal with it anymore; it's killing us."

Cheering soared, and I agreed with her. Every morning was an ordeal to pack my stuff while it was raining and barely light outside. Meanwhile, it was October and the temperature was dropping, which didn't make it fun to get out of your sleeping bag. On the other hand, I understood the City Council's viewpoint. Nowhere else had I seen such sloppy people as with the homeless. They lived as if the whole world belonged to them, disregarding the need to maintain their surroundings. Garbage constantly piled up around their tents, and city workers were left to clean it up.

Natasha grabbed the microphone and went to stand at the podium in front of the room. "We've suffered enough injustice; we have to work till we collapse. Employers exploit us. We work for peanuts as the price of food and housing are rising at an alarming rate."

I frowned. Was it true employers exploited their employees? Did employers not have rules to follow? My father had his own business, and I had always heard the other side of the story: that employees didn't want to work hard and they thought only about their rights and not their responsibilities. Natasha was right that the cost of living was not in balance with the minimum hourly wage being paid. It all depended on which side of the line you were on, whether at the top or the bottom, I decided. My father worked day and night while his employees went home at 4 p.m. It's only logical he made more than them as he carried more responsibility.

I once heard a co-worker in the supermarket where I worked say, 'I'm just a worker who shows up and that's it. I've no opinion, I just have to work for my money whether I like it or not.'

In the meantime, Natasha stormed on, "Employers and landlords can send you packing without giving any reason. Nobody is listening to us. They are swimming in their own money. They have no understanding of our situation."

Approving cries rose from the group which had formed around her. I looked around the table where I was sitting. Rinc's face was flushed; he clearly agreed with Natasha.

Jaxsen sat there, taken aback. He looked at me and leaned in closer. He tried to be heard above the noise.

"Do you agree with Natasha?" he asked.

"Not totally," I said hesitantly.

"I totally don't," he said. "I know from my own experience that you can do well when you work hard."

"You're right," I agreed. "But what if there are no opportunities to get ahead of the game? What if you, just like me, can't find a better job than working in a fast-food restaurant?"

He nodded. "You can become desperate and blame somebody else for your misfortune or keep trying to improve your situation," he said, shrugging.

I had to agree with him.

"We have to act!" screamed Natasha. "We have to let the authorities know they can't mess with us!"

A volunteer from the shelter realized that the situation was escalating. He took over the mic from Natasha and urged the people to calm down. They ignored him, and the screaming only grew louder.

"Okay, ladies and gentlemen," the volunteer warned loudly through the mic, "this is the last time I'll ask. If you quiet down now, you can stay; otherwise, you have to go outside and talk there. If you're too noisy there, you'll have the police on your tail. Tell me what you prefer."

"Okay, okay," people mumbled, and everybody returned to their seats. Slowly, the room quieted down, and when a volunteer started playing the piano, the atmosphere shifted.

The mic volunteer took Natasha aside. I could see that he tried to stay calm but still reprimanded her for agitating the group.

Later that evening, Rinc, Amy, and I walked back to the park. "Natasha will not be allowed in the shelter anymore if she continues like she did this evening," said Rinc. "The man who took the mic away from her said she should talk to the city council."

"Seems to me like a much better option than screaming," I couldn't resist saying.

It earned me an angry look from Rinc, but Amy agreed with me.

At the same time, in early October, as the homeless people struggled with their collective situation, the stores prepared for Thanksgiving. Large orange pumpkins were harvested from the land, offered for sale, and displayed in stores in square cardboard boxes that reached my waist. The smell of freshly baked pumpkin pies filled the streets, and frozen turkeys sold for a dollar per pound.

In the shelter, a special dinner was served. The atmosphere among the attendees was harmonious. The turkey was more tender than I remembered from the year before. Additionally, the cranberry sauce and stuffing tasted better. With the carrots, peas, Brussels sprouts, and corn, my plate became a vibrant display of colors. I feasted on this delicious food, thankful I didn't have to cook it entirely by myself this year.

A volunteer from the shelter took the mic during the dinner. "Please take a couple of minutes to think about what you're thankful for and then tell the people at your table," he said. "I myself am grateful we have so many guests tonight who came for the Thanksgiving dinner."

For a moment, it was quiet at my table. We looked at each other, curious to see who would speak first.

"I'll start," Amy said finally, sitting up a bit straighter. "I'm not thankful for the bad weather of the last few weeks," she began and the others around the table mumbled in agreement. "But," she continued, "I am grateful for Tristan and Isolde and that you guys," she looked around the circle, "are my friends."

Again, approving mumbling followed.

The others said that they were happy with the shelter and thankful for their health. Jaxsen announced he had become a grandfather a couple of weeks ago. Then it was my turn. I too was grateful for the shelter and the volunteers, for my new friends, and for my health.

"I'm especially happy I dared to take the step to another life," I said.

There was a brief silence, and five pairs of eyes stared at me. I sensed them thinking: if she's thankful for this life, then the life she had before must have been even worse.

Jaxsen broke the uncomfortable silence and raised his glass. "To everyone who's thankful for the little things in life. Because," he continued, "happiness doesn't make you thankful, but thankfulness makes you happy."

We clinked our coffee cups and lemonade glasses together to toast that proclamation.

25. Halloween

With Thanksgiving behind us, orange pumpkins once again took centre stage, now repurposed to ward off supposed evil spirits. Their stems became handles, their pulp scooped from their fat bellies. Assisted by their parents, little artists carved faces into the orange walls using razor-sharp kitchen knives. Proudly, the children placed their grinning creations at the front door and lit candles inside their hollowed insides.

Before Boy and I went to the park to sleep, we often walked around the nearby neighbourhood. Glowing jack-o'-lantern eyes stared at us from the gardens. Black spiderwebs and white ghosts hung in front of house windows. Gardens were suddenly transformed into cemeteries, with 'Rest in Peace' written on lopsided tombstones.

An uncomfortable atmosphere hung over the city. I often looked over my shoulder only to find nothing behind me. Sometimes the hairs on my neck stood up suddenly and goosebumps crept over my arms. When I looked around, I didn't see anything unusual, but I was sure something was nearby. It didn't help that I knew Victoria was one of the most significant witchcraft centres in the world. What had possessed me to come here in the first place? The weather? To be as far away from family as possible? At this point, I was beginning to worry I had gotten myself into something worse.

During one of my walks, I stumbled upon a garden with a fake child's grave. Astonished, I stood stock-still. In front of the tombstone, a child's hand seemed to emerge from the ground. The house, a cottage, was dark. Vines wound around the veranda where a pumpkin with a flickering light stood, seemingly smirking. The garden was overgrown, with several tombstones scattered in the tall grass. What kind of monsters lived behind the door of this haunted house, mocking dead babies? The image of Hansel and Gretel and the witch entered my mind. I could almost hear the squeaky voice of the old woman as she poked the crackling fire of the oven. The children wailed and begged, but she didn't give in. A man with a dog walked past behind me. Boy sniffed at the dog. The man looked at me as if to say: 'Mind your own business; in this neighbourhood, we decide for ourselves what is acceptable.'

Halloween night began, and groups of children in costumes roamed the city. Everywhere I walked with Boy through the streets, I ran into them. At houses with lights on, the children rang doorbells and called out, "Trick or treat," as someone opened the door. With bags full of candy, they darted through the dark to the next house.

I couldn't help but remember yesterday's newspaper headline: *'Police Warn About Sharp Objects in Candy'*. Would the evening turn into a nightmare for these happy children when they tasted Snickers and Kitkats?

Apparently, I wasn't the only one thinking about this. As I walked by a school parking lot, I noticed rows of cars with their trunks open.

"What is going on here?" I asked a mother standing at one of the cars.

"Didn't you read about the razors and needles in the candy in the newspaper?" she replied accusatorily.

"Yes, I read about it," I said, "but what's that got to do with all these people here?"

"A group of parents decided to celebrate Halloween here. This way, we can ensure the children get safe candy," she explained.

I nodded. "Have fun," I said and continued walking along the sidewalk by the parking lot. Were all these people really honest and trustworthy? Were they so naive? Had they forgotten about the father who, years ago, filled candy with poison to kill his own son and collect insurance money? How could one differentiate the good parents from the bad ones? What criteria had been set for acceptance into this group?

Suddenly, memories of the past flooded my mind. On Halloween, I used to go trick-or-treating with my brother and sister in the neighbourhood. We collected bags full of candy. At home, I would hide my candy behind a pile of clothes in my bedroom closet; not just because of my siblings...

Rage and scorn welled up in me as I recalled one afternoon after Halloween. I came home from school to find my mother in her usual spot on the couch, digging her fat hand into a big bag of candy; my bag of candy!

"That bag is mine," I said, my fury barely restrained.

"Sorry," my mother replied indifferently, "you can't eat it all by yourself anyway."

Oh, how I hated her at that moment. I didn't say anything; I just snatched the bag with the last few candies left from her hands. She called after me, accusing me of being rude for taking the candy away like that.

A few days later, she tried the same thing with my brother and sister. They didn't stand for it and lashed out at her, calling her names. She retreated onto the couch, whimpering and crying, lamenting about her difficult life. That was the moment when any remaining shreds of respect I had for her vanished completely.

26. A place to settle

A week later, at the beginning of November, I began to view my street life and that of my fellow homeless people in a different light.

In the morning, I went to work as usual. Customers streamed in, and Sandra and I darted back and forth, ensuring each order reached the right person. Exhausted, I headed to the library after work. I worked on my story for a few hours until fatigue finally claimed me. Despite having a well-formed story, I found myself stuck. I couldn't endlessly rant about my work, the struggles of homelessness, and the shelter. Maybe doing more volunteer work at the shelter would provide additional material for my writing.

With limited material to write about, I decided to help prepare dinner at the shelter. I put my tablet away, said goodbye to the librarian, and left the building. Outside, the rain drizzled down. I pulled my hoodie over my head, already dreading the task of setting up my tent that night.

The library wasn't far from the shelter, and within five minutes, I walked into the building. The warmth was a welcome contrast to the cold drizzle outside. I headed straight for the main hall. Pausing at the threshold, I surveyed the room in surprise. What was going on here? Everyone seemed to be engaged in animated conversations. Was this some kind of celebration?

I walked over to Jaxsen, who was sitting at a table near the door. "What's going on?" I asked. "It looks like a celebration."

"That's right," Jaxsen replied with a grin. "We have something to celebrate."

"Whose birthday is it?" I asked, scanning the room for the guest of honor.

Jaxsen laughed. "It's nobody's birthday, but this morning Alex wasn't chased away."

"What do you mean?" I asked, puzzled.

Jaxsen pointed towards the centre of the room. There, amidst a group of people, stood Alex—the bearded man I had met a few weeks before. He was the one who had been talking to Jayden during the fight with Amy.

"Not chased away? What do you mean by that?" I asked again.

Jaxsen explained, "Alex's tent was set up on the courthouse lawn, and this morning, the bylaw officer told him, 'The rules for the local parks don't apply to the garden and lawn around the provincial courthouse. The courthouse is on provincial land. You can leave your tent up.'"

Initially, I didn't see the significance of this until Jaxsen's explanation sank in. This statement meant that we had found a permanent camping spot! We no longer had to dismantle our tents in the mornings, and we could even sleep in if we wanted to. The courthouse was centrally located, close to both the shelter and my work. It meant I wouldn't have to lug my backpack around as much.

I was thrilled by the news. I felt lighter and more optimistic. The sense of unity at the shelter during dinner that evening gave me new energy. While our problems were far from resolved, our outlook had certainly improved.

After dinner, Natasha asked for the mic. Overflowing with enthusiasm and barely containing her sparkling energy, she waved the mic in one hand while gesticulating wildly with the other.

"Tonight, I invite everybody to set up your tents on the lawn in front of the courthouse," she began.

A cheer rose from the crowd, but immediately, some hands shot up. "The city will surely not accept it if we all go there together," someone yelled.

"You're right," Natasha agreed, "and that's exactly the objective. At this moment, no one has the right to send us away from there. If they want us to leave, they'll have to negotiate with us. That's why I need people who will work with me to draft terms and conditions that the city must satisfy before we leave the courthouse lawn. Are there any volunteers who, like me, want to be spokespeople for our group?"

The homeless people looked at each other. Most seemed hesitant about taking on the responsibility Natasha was asking for. A few hands went up. Natasha told the rest of the group she would keep them updated on the developments. She then took a seat with the volunteers at a separate table. Pulling out a notebook and a pen, she began jotting down notes as the small group delved into discussion.

Shortly after, the homeless crowd left the shelter in small groups. Amy, Rinc, and I headed to the courthouse. We agreed we should at least give it a try and sleep there for a night.

By the time we arrived at our new camping spot, a few tents were already set up. There was space for at least a hundred tents on the lawn, and that first evening, about ten were already in place. We picked a spot not too far from the street but away from the nearby parking lot. By the light of the streetlamps, we set up our tents; mine nestled between Amy's and Rinc's.

Rinc was thrilled about the prospect of being able to sleep in the next morning. I couldn't help but laugh.

"This is very serious business, huh?" he said with a grin.

"I totally agree, but I think it's funny," I replied.

I wasn't entirely sure if 'funny' was the right word. 'Nervously stressed about what the future would bring' might have been a better description.

We made a fire in the middle of the vast lawn, and other tent dwellers came over to join us. Cowboy Hat had also set up his tent. He arrived with long sticks and a tarp, setting up an awning over the fire so we could sit out of the rain. He gave me a wink. Now that he was showing his helpful side, he didn't seem quite as much of a creep. Still, I was glad I wasn't sitting beside him.

A hopeful, harmonious expectancy hung in the air. We felt we could conquer the world and made plans on how we would persuade the city council to meet our demands. Nevertheless, we were certain that the city wouldn't tolerate our presence without a fight. They would look for any loophole to get rid of us.

The next morning, we weren't awakened by the bylaw officer. For the homeless people who didn't have to go anywhere, this must have felt like a wonderful turn of events. For me, however, it was different; I had to go to work. Fortunately, my internal clock was set for 7 a.m., and I woke up only 15 minutes later than usual. If I had slept in, I would have had a significant problem; keeping my job was essential. For the following mornings, I set an alarm on my phone to ensure I wouldn't be late.

27. Haunting lies

By now it had been two months since I had left home and I hadn't heard anything from my parents, brother, or my sister. I only knew what Pete told me on Facebook. I was happy and sad at the same time: happy because I didn't have to hang around them anymore but sad about everything that could have been different. It was disappointing to realize that I apparently wasn't important enough for them to ask Pete about my circumstances.

I had contact with Pete regularly when I was in the library writing my story. Now that the days were growing shorter and I didn't have to hurry to the park to set up my tent before dark, I went to the library three evenings a week, as it was open until 9 p.m. on Tuesdays, Wednesdays, and Thursdays. I always looked forward to the conversations with Pete.

"What's up?" he usually wrote.

"Nothing," I would say, and then I would write a narration about all the events we had experienced over the last couple of days. When I realized what 'nothing' actually meant, I had to grin. Maybe Pete did the same. I could only guess. He rarely used smiley faces. However, he sometimes surprised me with his witty comebacks. I thought he had a good sense of humour. The conversations we had were warm, bright spots in the life I mostly spent outside in the cold.

Pete had given up on coming to Victoria. His father's health didn't improve, so he wasn't able to work. If Pete were to leave, his parents wouldn't have any income.

"I don't have the heart to do it," he wrote.

The relationships at his home had improved now that he had taken on so much responsibility. His parents seemed to appreciate his dedication and were now accepting of his painting in his free time.

"I've submitted a couple of paintings to the Art Show in the community centre," he wrote.

I was happy for him. It looked like his life was back on track. Somewhere, something stung. Was I jealous? Did I want to change places with him? No. I decided immediately; that wasn't what I wanted. I didn't want to go back to Saskatoon, back to my family, and even not back to my supermarket job. Determined, I plunged into my story.

Maybe the old man, sitting at the other side of the table reading a book, saw my resolute face, or perhaps he saw my fingers racing madly over the keyboard because he asked, "Is everything going well, young lady?"

I looked up and nodded. I was just in the middle of a sentence and continued writing. "Thanks," I quickly said as politely as possible.

A beep told me there was a message coming in on Facebook. "Did you find housing yet?" asked Pete.

That was an annoying question. Of course, I had a place to live, but did he expect me to call my tent a living space? I wanted to lie, but that didn't feel right. How could I explain I had a permanent place without saying it was just a tent?

"Yes," I wrote, "I've found a spot to live. Rinc and Amy live close by. The city has appointed this spot to us. We also have a big field as a front yard. The neighbours often make a campfire at night. I regularly go over there to drink something and have a chat."

Before I sent the message, I read it over at least three times. Could Pete, as an outsider, infer from this what I really meant? Could he see through my lies? I felt nauseous. I was deceiving my best friend.

"Nice, eh," Pete wrote. "What's your address?"

Again such a difficult question. If I gave him the address of the courthouse, he would easily be able to find out where I was hanging out. Google Maps was, at this moment, my enemy.

"It doesn't make much sense to give you my address," I wrote, "it's just temporary. I'm on the list for another, somewhat bigger place. This is only one room."

Was I lying? Officially, I hadn't applied for other housing; however, the city was looking for a solution for all of the homeless people. Or had I told a half-truth? I didn't know if there was a difference between lies and half-truths. What I did know was that I was ashamed that my life still wasn't in order and that, after two months, it didn't look anything like what I had hoped for. I was involved with people I didn't really want to associate with. I had bragged that life would improve when I left home, but in reality, I needed assistance from others, such as my employer and the shelter. I had to admit that I couldn't really manage by myself in a big city and that I had taken it too lightly.

I ended the conversation with the excuse that I didn't want to walk home too late through the dark. After that, I worked for another hour on my story, and because of my sombre mood, the story also took on a sombre tone. It felt like I lost a friend tonight, and it was my own fault. To win him back, I would have to tell the truth. And the truth was hard.

I was so ashamed of my lies that I didn't even consider confessing them. Pete wasn't even aware our relationship had developed a fracture. I still had time before coming clean. I put my tablet in my bag. "See you later," I said to the old man.

"See you next time," he replied.

Outside, the street glistened under the streetlights. Car tires splashed through the puddles. The wind blew a drizzly rain in my face and soaked my clothes. I tucked into my coat and walked the few streets to the courthouse. My shoes made a squishing sound when I walked over the wet grass to my tent. Amy and her dogs were nowhere to be seen. They were probably already sleeping. Boy was lying in front of my tent and jumped up. With his tail wagging, he walked toward me. I hugged him. His fur was wet and sticky.

From the campfire, I heard Rinc calling my name.

"Come, Boy," I said, "let's dry ourselves out a bit by the fire." The mood in the circle around the fire was cheerful. I smelled the sweet scent of marijuana. I sank on a small stool. Boy lay down at my feet, close to the fire. I stared into the flames, feeling distracted. I was surrounded by laughter. The drug had a cheerful effect on the people.

Somebody squatted down beside me and put an arm around my shoulders. Startled, I looked up and into Cowboy Hat's black eyes. My heart raced as I tried to pull away from under his arm.

"Calm down, girlie," he said soothingly. He offered me a joint. "Take a puff; it'll make you feel better. I think you could use it."

I stared at the joint and back to his black eyes. Did I imagine it, or did they look friendly? Was he right? Would it make me feel better? I could try it just once. I had already done so many dumb things tonight; one more wouldn't make a difference.

I took his joint from him. With hesitation, I glanced at Cowboy Hat's face. Was that the familiar cunning smile around his mouth again?

"Go ahead," he encouraged me.

I took a puff and gave the joint back. The smoke tickled my throat and lungs. I coughed. We both laughed about it. Cowboy Hat also took a puff and handed the joint back to me.

This time it went better. Slowly, the world became happier and more relaxed. Everything would be okay.

Cowboy Hat threw the last piece of the joint into the fire.

"I'm going to my tent," I decided.

Cowboy Hat stood up. "I'll walk with you."

I let him, and together we walked the path to my tent. Boy followed us.

"Good night, missy," Cowboy Hat said. His hand ever so slightly touched my face. Vaguely, I was aware of the strange situation, but the weed had made me carefree.

"Till tomorrow," he whispered close to my ear.

"That's enough," I heard Rinc's voice behind me.

Cowboy Hat turned towards Rinc and slowly backed up, returning to the fire. How was it possible, I thought, that Cowboy Hat stepped aside for Rinc, who was a lot smaller than him? I didn't think long about it before crawling into my tent. Boy shook himself and also came inside. Rinc squatted in from of my tent door.

"You have to be more careful, Nadia," he hissed, "you can't trust that guy."

"Okay," I answered absently and zipped the door shut in front of his nose. I heard him mumble something, but I didn't catch what he said. That night, I slept without a worry for the first time since arriving in Victoria.

28. Shivering cold

The tent encampment grew. Newspaper articles about our camp reached the front pages. From cities all over the island and even from the mainland, the homeless came to Victoria to live in the 'tent city'. The Victoria homeless people seemed to relax now they didn't have to drag their stuff around the city all day long. Daily, we got new neighbours, and the camp started to look terribly messy and overcrowded. Some handy men dragged old building materials to the camp and put wooden dwellings together They weren't as beautiful as the tiny houses I saw on Pinterest, but they provided better protection against the rain and the wind than my army tent.

To give our tents extra protection against the water that had been coming down daily for so long, Rinc and I draped big blue, green, and grey tarps over our tents and Amy's. Still, it wasn't very comfortable in my tent. My sleeping bag and clothes were wet and cold from the continuous humidity, and they didn't even dry at night by the campfire. I knew the island had a temperate rainforest climate, but I had no idea what that meant when I decided to travel here. Fortunately, the temperature wasn't anything to complain about. In November, it hadn't gone below seven degrees Celcius yet.

"Tonight we'll have frost," announced Brian, one of the tent city residents. It was one of the last days of November. We sat around the campfire and warmed our hands. The sky was clear, and the moon cast a blue-white glow over the tents. The rain clouds were gone, and a cold east wind made us shiver in our damp clothes.

I layered my clothes, crawled into my sleeping bag, and covered myself with all the blankets I had. Boy lay tight against me. I had gotten used to his sighs and sniffs.

Despite my efforts, my nose and my cheeks were ice cold when I woke up the next morning. I didn't have much desire to climb out of my sleeping bag, but I had no choice. I had to go to work. At least, at McDonald's it was warm, I told myself.

Reluctantly, I unzipped my tent. The puddles on the path were covered with a thin layer of ice. I wrapped an extra blanket around my shoulders and crawled out of my tent. For a moment, I considered making a fire in the brazier Rinc had brought a couple of days ago. I didn't, though. Who knew how long it would take until Rinc woke up? There was a good chance the fire would go out. It would be a waste of wood if nobody enjoyed the warmth.

In the meantime, I ate a dry muffin and gave Boy his kibble. Shivering from the cold, I looked around to see if anybody else was awake yet, but the camp was still quiet. I was one of the few who had a job and left early. Between the tents was an immense mess; garbage was strewn everywhere. I started to wonder what was wrong with these people. Why didn't they throw their garbage into the cans provided by the city? Some residents took care of their small spaces, but overall, the encampment gave the impression that we were living on a rubbish dump.

The tent city drew a lot of attention now that it was getting really cold. People from all over the city brought us blankets, warm clothes, and food. Members of the Christ Church Cathedral, the Anglican church across from the courthouse, brought home-baked cookies. They were delicious.

Passers-by took pictures, and TV crews filmed us. I did my best to avoid the photographers and especially the TV people. I absolutely did not want to be in the newspaper or on TV like Rinc, who told his story to a newspaper journalist, or like Natasha, who appeared on the evening news. Early in the mornings, I went to the fast-food restaurant; the afternoons I spent either in the library or at the shelter. I waited for dark before heading back home to my tent.

I didn't see Amy much. She crawled into her sleeping bag as soon as dusk set in and came out long after I was gone. In the middle of the night, I heard her coughing; a raw cough that didn't go away. I was worried about her.

"Lord," I prayed, "could You please make her better? Or maybe not, she then has to suffer even longer. Or maybe yes, because I don't know where she'll go when she dies. Actually, You'll have to decide what is best," I ended my jumbled prayer.

29. Renewed hope

The library was only two blocks away from the courthouse. I gratefully used the free Internet to look up facts I was using in my story.
One evening, a librarian approached me. She took a seat at my table.
"I'm Shanna," she said, shaking my hand.
"Nadia," I replied.
"I see you here so often," she said, "and you're always typing. Are you studying a certain topic for school, or are you a writer?"
"I'm writing my story," I told her.
"You must have gone through a lot, given how much you're writing," Shanna said.
"Maybe, yes," I smiled, "but I also write down my opinions about certain situations. It's not only the events I describe."
"I see," she nodded. "Are you going to publish it someday?"
"Maybe," I kept my options open.
"Beautiful," she said, "I would love to read it." She stood up. "If you need anything, information you can't find, feel free to ask."
"I'll do that," I said.
For a moment, I stared quietly ahead. I pondered how many people had come into my life since I had broken away from my old life. I felt thankful for the attention people gave me and the interest some had in what I was doing. In my head, I built a list of friendly people who could potentially help if needed or whom I could ask for advice.

"May I sit at your table again?" said a voice, pulling me out of my deep contemplation.

I looked up and saw the old man who often sat at my table. He had a pile of books in his hands.

"Of course," I said welcomingly.

The old man sat down. He laid the books in front of him on the table. One by one, he looked at them, as if he didn't know which one to read first. His hands caressed the covers.

I continued typing. I looked up when I got stuck with my story. My gaze rested on the old man who was seated opposite me. He had hung his long, dark blue raincoat over the chair beside him; his hat lay in front of him on the table. He sat straight up and flipped through the yellowed pages of a booklet. His fingers slid slowly from top to bottom over the pages. His hands were old, with dark spots on the pale skin.

It was nearly closing time, so I got ready to put my tablet away. The old man followed my example and closed the yellowed book. He held on to the table as he stood up. He pushed his chair under the table precisely, picked up the pile of books and his hat, nodded at me, and walked to the exit.

Suddenly, he seemed to change his mind and took a couple of steps back to the table.

"Do you find it easier to study here than at home?" he asked.

I don't know why, maybe he radiated enough trustworthiness or reminded me of my grandpa, but I blurted out, "I have no home, and I'm not studying."

He looked at me, took his glasses from his nose, and rubbed his eyes.

"In any case, you're typing pretty fast, whatever you're doing."

"I'm writing my story," I said.

"Good," he said pensively. He added, "When you're ready to publish it, I would love to proofread it for you."

I stared at him and felt myself becoming shy. Tonight, he was the second person to ask me about my writing. I hadn't seriously thought about sharing my story with anybody. That was a little bit scary.

"I'm writing a lot of personal things," I said. "I don't know if I dare let somebody read it."

"Good," he said again. "Keep writing as if nobody will ever read it. That way your deepest emotions will come to the surface. That speaks to potential readers. They will recognize themselves in it. And," he added, "if you still think it's too scary," and he smiled, "you can always publish it under a pseudonym."

I nodded. That was not such a bad idea. That way I wouldn't have to be afraid of offending somebody or being hurt. People would only criticize the work of the author.

"Thank you," I said and picked up my bag.

"If you need help, you can always ask me. I come here often. Sitting between the books is like sitting between old friends, plus the ladies here know me."

I looked behind me at the front desk. Shanna nodded at us.

"Thank you very much," I said again and walked to the exit where Boy was waiting for me. I put some kibble in his bowl. After he had finished eating, we headed off to the tent city. I saw the old man walking in the opposite direction and wondered who he was.

I pondered the idea of publishing my story. It seemed more and more intriguing to me, and I started to feel excited. Out of pure joy, I bopped Boy jovially on his head, and he barked, startled. I knelt beside him on the sidewalk and hugged him. He licked my hands and my face until I'd had enough.

Light-hearted, I walked back to the tent encampment. I had a job and a project to work on. Add a normal living space to it and nothing could hurt me anymore.

30. Website

Back in the tent city, I heard Natasha arguing heatedly. She sat on a lawn chair in the circle around the campfire.

"They can't take us away from here," she yelled. "We have the right to stay here with our tents. Some of us have had years of physical and mental stress because we've had to break up our camps every day and wander through the city. We've never had a place to rest. Now everything has changed, and we're going to take care of our physical and emotional well-being. We finally have a home, a community, and safety."

From a distance, I stood still and tried to follow what the others in the group were saying.

Alex brought up the idea that we should explain our points of view on the Internet. "We need a website," he shouted, "then everybody can read what our ideas are, and we can offer a counter-argument against the deception the newspaper is publishing and against the slander from neighbours in online forums."

His idea gained approval.

"We need somebody who can write the text for the website," Natasha said. "Who wants to volunteer?"

Several hands went up, but I could tell by the look on Natasha's face that she didn't see any suitable candidates.

"Do you have a computer?" she asked each of them. One by one, they shook their heads. Only an older man with a long grey beard had a laptop. Natasha looked doubtful.

I spotted Rinc among the people sitting around the fire. Our eyes met, and I saw a light inside of him switch on.

No, I thought, no, not that.

I wildly shook my head, but he stood up and pointed towards me. "Nadia is a good writer," he shouted to Natasha, "she's always writing."

Suddenly, all eyes were on me. Natasha asked, "Is that right? Are you a good writer?"

"Maybe," I said, biting back my frustration.

Questioningly, she looked at me. "What kind of answer is that? You're going to help me with the text," she decided resolutely.

"Why do you think I want that?" I asked rudely.

"What did you say? You're part of this community too, right? We can only accomplish something when we work together. We can't achieve anything through laziness. We all have to use our talents to help each other. Some are building new shelters, others are talking to the city council, and others, such as yourself, can help with the wording of our terms and conditions and writing the text for our new website."

Natasha kept on rambling and succeeded gloriously in making me feel guilty. I felt like a fool in front of the men listening around the campfire. She completely ignored my objections. She walked towards me, her thick, dark, curly hair dancing on her shoulders.

"Can we get started now?" she asked.

I shrugged indifferently and sat in the circle. I pulled out my tablet and turned it on. The battery was almost full. Too bad. By the flickering light of the fire, I typed what she dictated to me. She continuously repeated herself. I wrote it down anyway. Later on, I would edit or delete it. I was afraid that drafting up the terms and conditions and writing the website text would demand a lot of my free time.

"On what website will this text be placed?" I asked without thinking.

"That website hasn't been created yet, right?" Natasha said impatiently.

"Oh, crap," I sighed, seeing the storm coming. "Who is going to make the website?" Dumb question, of course, because I already knew the answer.

"Do you know how to make a website?" Natasha asked.

"No, never done one," I said shortly.

"But you could figure it out, right?" she pressed on.

I sighed and said, "But you only talked about the writing of the text, and now suddenly you're adding building a website to it."

"Do you think," she hissed close to my ear, "that I can find somebody in this bunch of scum who is civilized and intelligent enough to make a website? Someone who isn't wasting time on drugs, procrastination, self-indulgence, or simply going with the flow?"

I shrugged. I didn't have much confidence in the others either.

"You're a winning lottery ticket," she grinned. She firmly put her arm around me and pulled me close. The rickety chair I was sitting on almost flipped upside down. I could barely support myself with my left hand on the muddy grass. Bah! I swiped my hand as cleanly as possible on my jacket. Natasha still held me tightly, her face close to mine. She almost looked like she was in love with me, and I thought: you're not right in your head; something's wrong with you.

Natasha continued ranting while I typed. My eyes got tired from staring at the screen, where reflections of the fire danced. All of a sudden, I was done.

"Where are the others who applied for this job?" I asked, irritated.

"Oh, those," Natasha said wearily. "They threw in the towel. Just like I said, they're busy doing nothing."

"I'm going to bed," I said, putting my tablet in my bag. "I have to work tomorrow and need to wake up early."

"You're working?" Natasha said, surprised. "There's more to you than I initially realized."

"Thank you," I said sarcastically and stared at her until she began shifting uncomfortably in her chair. I stood up and, without saying another word, walked to my tent. I loathed it when people only took into account the outside of a person.

31. Caught

A couple of days later, around 4 p.m., what I had feared, happened. The temperature was close to zero. Shivering, I stood by the campfire. My wet clothes hadn't dried at all. The skin of my feet was soaked and mushy from walking in wet shoes for days. Amy and Rinc sat drowsily, buried deep in their blankets. The three dogs lay close to the fire. I sat, ruminating on the bleakness of my situation.

Dusk was coming. Behind me was the path that wound around the tents.

"Good afternoon," a voice said.

I turned and looked straight into the enormous lens of a camera. I quickly turned back to the fire.

"May I ask you something?" asked the voice behind the camera.

"What's your question?" I said, with my back turned to the voice.

"Are you the one maintaining the website for the tent city?" asked the voice.

"I'm involved with the website, yes," I said.

"May I know your name?" asked again the voice.

"No," I said briskly.

"How long have you been homeless and how long have you been living here?"

"I'm not homeless, and I've lived here since the beginning of November," I said.

Why, I complained to myself, am I answering?

The man behind the voice understood that I wasn't eager to answer his questions. After thanking me, he walked further along to the next campfire where Natasha's group was mingling. I soon heard Natasha frantically lecturing the man. I saw her pointing at me, and the next thing I knew the camera swung in my direction. I turned back to our fire.

Until the early evening, the man walked through the camp and interviewed several of my neighbours. As he was leaving the camp, he walked past my tent again. I was sitting with Amy by the fire. I had opened a can of beans in tomato sauce and was warming the contents in a pot above the fire. The cameraman looked at me and nodded politely. I followed him with my eyes until he reached the street. I would loved to have taken away his camera and deleted the section with me on it. Was he going to put the video on YouTube or, worse, were we going to be on TV?

A couple of days later, I would find out the answer.

When I entered the encampment in the afternoon, Rinc met me at the entrance.

"Hi Nadia," he said.

"Hi Rinc," I replied.

I looked at him, scanning his demeanor. Something about it made me suspicious. "Since when are you the welcoming committee?"

"Look, I was thinking, I wanted to meet you halfway," he began. He stood in the middle of the path, blocking my way. He shifted from one foot to the other, holding his shoulders high as if he were very cold. He wrapped his arms around himself and rubbed them to get warm.

"What's the matter?" I asked, suspicious. Why didn't he let me through, and since when was he feeling so cold? He was used to living outside. Something must have happened.

"You have a visitor," he blurted, "I wanted to let you know before you go any further."

A paralyzing feeling dropped from my stomach into my legs.

"Is it somebody from home?" I asked, looking at Rinc with frightened eyes.

"Your father," Rinc whispered. He glanced over his shoulder toward our tents.

Indeed, my father stood in front of my tent, warming his hands by the fire that Amy and Rinc kept burning all day long.

I had hoped after he attempted to stop me at the station in Saskatoon, that he would have given up his search. He was more persistent than I thought he would be. What could be behind his decision to come all the way to Victoria to find me? Fatherly love?

I laughed with contempt.

"What is it?" Rinc asked.

"Nothing," I said, "just a thought that came to me."

Was he going to try to take me back to Saskatchewan? Was there a law I didn't know about that could grant him that right? Lightning-fast, I recalled the excerpts I had read on the Internet about maturity. I couldn't remember anything that would give him the right to take me back. Still, I considered the possibility. I had lived under so much pressure for so long that I sometimes felt other people had the right to control me, to force me to do things I didn't want to do; that I had no say in my own life.

"Can he force me to go home with him?" I asked Rinc, scared.

Rind shook his head. "He doesn't have that right. You're an adult. No law can enforce you to go back with him."

I inhaled deeply, walked past Rinc, and followed the muddy path that led to our tents. I walked until I stood in front of my father, the fire safely between us.

"Hi," I said shortly, clenching my teeth.

"Hi Nadia," he said stiffly.

I didn't ask how he knew I was here. The incident with the cameraman had been haunting my thoughts continuously for the last few days.

"Why are you doing this to me?" my father burst out, waving an arm toward the jumble of tents.

"What?" I exclaimed in utter surprise. I gasped for air. "I'm not doing anything to anybody. Always somebody did something to me. Now suddenly you're going to play the victim? Be happy you got rid of me!" I stood there, my legs trembling.

"Happy?" he said, surprised. "Why would I be happy if I never saw my daughter again?"

I was perplexed. "First time I've heard you say that. I should have never been born, eh? You've certainly forgotten you said that."

"No, I haven't forgotten. I meant it when I said it, but not for the reason you think."

"What could be a good reason for such an awful statement?" I snapped angrily.

He was silent, and I taunted him, sneering. "Now you don't know what to say, eh?"

He nodded. "I would like to explain it. Privately."

He looked at Amy and Rinc, who sat huddled in their blankets by the fire. Only their eyes and part of their faces were uncovered. They pretended to be in their own worlds, but I knew they weren't missing a single word of the conversation.

"Let's go get a bite to eat somewhere," my father suggested.

Rinc looked at me and nodded almost imperceptibly.

For a moment, I didn't know what to do, then I gave in. "Okay," I said. "Let's go to Jake's Place."

I glanced over at Rinc, who seemed to understand the hint. If I needed help, he would know where to find me.

Silently, we walked the few blocks to the restaurant.

Once we were seated and had ordered from the menu, my father said, "Come home with me."

"My home is here," I replied. "I have a job, and my friends live here. In Saskatoon, there's nobody who cares for me. Except for Pete," I admitted. "And at home, they just use me as a slave. Those days are done."

My father was quiet for a while. He sipped his coffee and moved the salt and pepper shakers back and forth on the table.

"I asked Pete if he wanted to come visit you. I asked him because I thought he was your best friend. He didn't want to come."

"He can't come because his father is sick, and he has to do all the work," I explained.

"I know," said my father, "but that's not the real reason he refused to come with me. Their work is practically dead in the winter."

"What is the real reason, then?" I asked, worried.

"The real reason is that you lied to him. He trusted you, and you betrayed that trust."

"Since when have you had contact with Pete, and when does he tell you so much?" I demanded.

"Since the evening you left on the train," he answered. "I also have contact with his parents."

A wave of panic began to flood through me. The feeling made it hard for me to think clearly. I didn't want to lose Pete. He was the one I was closest to. He knew my classmates, the city I had lived in, and my family. My friends here weren't part of my history. Even though I hadn't known Pete for long, he had always been there. He had seen the situations in school and the city from a different perspective, but our situations were similar.

"Pete was the only one who was nice to me," I said. "I didn't want to tell him my ugly story. You'll see, soon I'll be gone from the tent city. Then I'll send him my address. Pete is the one who knows exactly how I feel because he has experienced the same things. He also comes from a terrible family."

The moment I said it, I felt a pang of sympathy for my father. Despite everything, he was the one who had been the least cruel to me. I understood that he had left my mother, but that statement about me not being born lingered painfully. I needed to understand why he had said that.

"You were going to explain why you thought I shouldn't have been born," I said, staring at him intently.

"I know I've given you far too little attention," he began apologetically. "I've been too preoccupied with making life comfortable for myself, which, as you know, didn't work out so well. Your mother knew I was planning to leave her. She knew before she got pregnant with you. We had agreed not to have any more children. I should have taken precautions myself, but I trusted her when she said she was using protection. She used the pregnancy to try and keep me with her. I stayed until you were born. Your grandmother came to stay with us the week before your delivery and was supposed to stay until your mother was on her feet. She scolded me about everything and more. In short, I was deemed a failure and not good enough for her daughter. I kept silent, but I had my plan ready. The day you were born, I left. I don't regret it. Living with your mother was impossible. I think we can agree on that," he added.

"You don't know what I think," I snapped. "You don't know what I've experienced and felt."

"I don't like telling you this," he said, "but I saw what was on your USB stick. I didn't read everything, but enough to know you were unhappy at home. I understood why you wanted to leave. I just didn't think you would actually do it."

I was silent. I had suspected my father might have snooped through the USB stick, but that wasn't surprising. What was surprising was learning how much my grandmother had opposed him. I had held her in high regard, but now I felt conflicted about her.

"I don't understand Grandma's behavior," I said. "She always protected me from Mom and the others. She knew how nasty they treated me and that Mom wasn't good for us. Why did she act like Mom was better than you?"

"That came later. She eventually realized that her daughter was using her youngest child as a doormat and took you under her wing. Unfortunately, Grandpa and Grandma lived too far away. I had considered asking them to take you in."

My jaw dropped in surprise. "Why didn't that happen?" I asked.

"Grandpa and Grandma had poor health. I thought it would have been too much for them."

"Too bad," I said simply, stirring my food with my fork.

"Years later, Grandma apologized to me when your mother sank deeper into her depression and refused to seek help."

I let the whole story sink in. I had never considered things from my father's perspective. I had always believed my version of events was the only one that mattered.

My father spoke again, breaking the silence. "If you decide to come back, you can stay with me. Your room is still ready."

I didn't answer immediately.

He understood that I wasn't going to accept his offer. He asked, "Can I help you find a place here?"

I shook my head. "Thanks for your offer, but I'll manage on my own."

"Good," he said, "I respect that. That's the real you again. Let's agree you don't let things get too far that you can't manage. Put your pride aside and call me if you need help."

What is 'too far', I wondered. In my father's eyes, I had already fallen too low, but in my own eyes, I was just beginning to rebuild my life. I was further along than when I had first arrived in Victoria two months ago.

My father paid the bill, and we walked back to the tent city, where we said our goodbyes. He was catching the last ferry to the mainland. In Saskatoon, the outdoor work was finished for the winter, but there was still enough work to do indoors. He hugged me tightly. I felt the unpleasantness of his bulging belly and his scraggly beard. A strange smell clung to him. Despite everything, I appreciated that he had come. He had traveled more than a thousand kilometres to find me. His visit gave me a renewed motivation to make something of my life. Or was it an urge to prove that I didn't need anyone from home? That I could live just fine without them?

32. He's got the whole world in His hands

December brought its usual challenges, as the days grew shorter and the streets were slick with rain. As the clock struck 4 p.m., the streetlights flickered on, casting their warm, yellow glow over the wet pavement. In the tent city, the residents huddled around the campfires whenever they weren't out in the city. The cold was relentless, and at night, sleep was elusive. I lay shivering in my tent, my feet and ankles numb from the cold and my nose perpetually running. The blankets and extra mats I scrounged for offered only marginal relief. It wasn't just the temperature that was harsh, but the pervasive humidity. Someone once told me that moist air is harder to heat than dry air, and now I knew it to be true.

Many others struggled with the same cold. A central fire was maintained all night, drawing people to its warmth. I often joined the group around the fire, where conversations were sparse and the heat was a welcome relief. Most of the time, people were wrapped tightly in their blankets, sleeping or half-awake. The flickering flames cast dancing shadows, obscuring faces and making it hard to recognize who was present.

One particular evening, I didn't realize that Cowboy Hat was sitting by the fire. I easily could have recognized him by his hat, but whether it was because of the flickering flames or because I just wasn't paying attention, I didn't see him until he sat up straight.

"Hey, missy," he said, looking over the flames. He lifted his hat and ran his hand through his long, black hair. A sensual grin appeared on his face, and he winked at me. I got scared. "Hi," I said and quickly looked around the circle to see if there might be somebody to save me from this prickly situation.

Fortunately, Brian was there so I sat down on the chair beside him. Boy lay down at my feet with his head on his paws. He sighed and enjoyed the warmth of the fire. I ignored Cowboy Hat by focusing on Brian. Deep furrows on his forehead gave him a worrisome appearance. A bunch of entangled dirty blonde curls and a grey beard framed his face. Whenever I talked to him during the day, he seemed confused, but whenever I met him at night at the fire, he was clear-headed. Brian knew everything about the stars. When the sky was clear of clouds, he was always looking up. Tonight, he told me about brown dwarfs and gas giants.

"Brown dwarfs," he said, "are smaller than stars but larger than gas giants. They form from the contraction of a cloud of gas, but the mass isn't enough to start proton fusion. Actually," he said in a confidential tone, "they're not brown at all but red. Brown dwarfs and gas giants are distinguished by their formation processes and their shapes."

I nodded and waited for him to continue.

"The first brown dwarf was discovered in 1995. Did you know that?"

"No," I said. "Please tell me more."

I liked listening to him, though, in the middle of the night, much of his educated chatter went over my head.

"The first brown dwarf located was Kelu-1. They discovered it in 1997," Brian continued, ignoring everybody around him. He talked about lithium and methane in brown dwarfs and

about temperatures measured in Kelvin. I had no clue how to convert that to Celsius or Fahrenheit, but I nodded along.
Brian shifted topics and talked about the smallest bacteria found earlier in the year.
"A long time ago, I worked at that laboratory," he said.
"What laboratory?" I asked.
"The one where they found the smallest bacteria," he replied.
"Where is that?" I asked again. He shouldn't assume that I knew everything.
"In California," he said somewhat impatiently.
"Oh, okay," I said. His answer still didn't clarify which lab he meant, but I let it go.
"I did research and sometimes was a guest speaker at the University of California."
"Oh," I said again. "Why aren't you teaching anymore?"
I wondered what happened to Brian. He had a sharp mind, and as far as I could see, he wasn't addicted to drugs. How had he ended up in a tent city in Victoria?
"It was all useless," he said.
"Useless?" I asked. It was frustrating to constantly drag words out of someone when the topic was personal, while they could talk endlessly about neutral subjects.
I waited for his response, turning my face towards him. Suddenly, he looked at me from under his bristly eyebrows with his sunken, old grey eyes. His breath formed small drops of condensation in his tangled beard.
"Look at the stars," he said. "See how vast they are. Consider that tiny bacteria in comparison. Reflect on your place in the grand scheme of the universe. We toil and slave away for a little money and comfort, only to die in the end."
"Well," I dared to say, "if you view it negatively, yes, you're right. There's no end to slaving for money. The wealthiest

people often hoard their money and always want more, while those with nothing give away what little they have."

Suddenly, I thought about Amy, who lost her money to Jayden. She had nothing and even the little she had was stolen. She remained calm, wasn't attached to the money, and even forgave Jayden for his theft.

"But, um…" I said as Brian remained silent. I gathered the courage to speak, though I wasn't entirely sure of my words. "If the universe is so endlessly big and bacteria so incomprehensibly small, don't you think there might be Someone who's holding us in His hands and controlling everything?"

The image of the Sunday school teacher from my grandparents' church flashed before my eyes. She used to teach us the well-known song, 'He's got the whole world in His Hands'.

Brian slowly turned his face towards me and observed me quietly. I waited anxiously for his reaction. Just as I thought he might have dropped the subject, he said, "I believe that somewhere, where I don't know, a God exists. But He's surely forgotten about me."

Tears sprang to my eyes. Pity for this good, old man filled my heart. Had God indeed forgotten him? It seemed so. An old man like Brian should be enjoying his retirement in an apartment, but instead, he was sitting in the middle of the night, shivering by a fire, surrounded by people who seemed lost. I didn't know what to say.

Not long after, Brian dozed off. Warmed by the fire, I stood up and crawled into my tent. Did God forget about all the people in the tent city? Was this literally a God-forsaken place? Deep down, I didn't believe that. There was still a glimmer of hope somewhere in my heart.

Boy cuddled against me, sighed deeply a few times, and soon fell asleep. Suddenly, I pinched my nose; Boy had let out one of his notorious farts. Quickly, I unzipped the tent door just a bit. Precious warmth escaped, and when the air was clear, I zipped the door shut again. I listened for a long time to the sounds surrounding my tent.

The next morning, I woke up stiff from the cold and with a growling stomach. I stumbled to the mobile bathrooms the city had placed near the camp and headed towards the warmth of the McDonald's restaurant.

33. Christmas parade

The whole city was bustling with preparations for the upcoming Christmas holidays. For four weeks, everything was in a state of commotion. People poured in and out of stores, searching for the perfect gifts for family and friends. Sometimes, dusk fell as early as 4 p.m., and well before dinner, people turned on their Christmas lights. The city was aglow with countless coloured lights. Historical buildings at the harbour and downtown were framed with thousands of twinkling lights. The eerie Halloween graves had been replaced by an abundance of sparkling Christmas figures. Some gardens were completely covered with reindeer, snowmen, and sleighs. Street blocks competed to see which residents had the most beautifully decorated garden. The stream of visitors had begun again. Tourists, their legs wrapped warmly in quilts, toured the city in horse-drawn carriages adorned with Christmas greenery, red bows, and a Santa Claus in the driver's seat. Even the horses wore Christmas hats. The entire city radiated warmth and coziness.

Thousands of visitors flocked downtown for the Christmas truckers' parade. I joined the crowd to see the vehicles decorated with lights, honking their way along the designated route. People stood in thick rows along the sidewalks, watching and waving to the passengers on the festively adorned trucks. The wheels of the vehicles sometimes splashed rainwater from the asphalt. I pulled my hoodie over my head and suddenly found myself like everyone else: wet coats and faces hidden under hoods.

Boy pressed himself against my legs, clearly not enjoying the blaring Christmas music from the loudspeakers on the trucks. Santa Claus was on the last truck. The crowd cheered, and many people joined the parade. I considered walking to the harbour where a boat parade was scheduled to sail by.

"Shall we walk with the parade?" I asked Boy. He looked at me with his faithful eyes, but I couldn't read an answer in them.

"You could also walk with me for a while," a voice said from beside me.

I turned and saw a pair of black eyes peering at me from under a cowboy hat.

No way! I thought. Not him again.

Boy pulled on the leash. "I'm going back to camp," I said, following Boy as he led the way. Cowboy Hat, with his long legs, had no trouble keeping up. I chose streets where there were more people, moving away from the larger crowd but still encountering enough folks heading to their cars.

"Why are you in such a hurry?" Cowboy Hat asked. "Can't we just smoke a joint somewhere?"

"I don't want that," I replied. "I've got to be at work on time tomorrow."

"Just one," he pleaded, tilting his head and looking at me questioningly.

He pulled a joint from the inside pocket of his coat and held it up to my nose. I caught a faint whiff of the sickly smell of marijuana. I remembered the evening at the campfire when we had smoked together and had some fun; how I had slept soundly and forgotten all my troubles. But the next morning, nothing had changed. I still had to go to McDonald's, and I still lived in the tent city. The drugs hadn't solved anything, and Rinc's warning about Cowboy Hat not being trustworthy echoed in my mind.

I shook my head. "No, I don't want a joint," I said firmly.

He didn't take no for an answer easily. He moved closer, putting an arm around my shoulders. I stopped and resolutely brushed his arm away. "Don't do that," I said, short of breath. Boy growled and bared his teeth.

I walked on. Cowboy Hat followed me for a few more metres before turning back toward the parade. At the corner of the block, I glanced back and saw him disappearing into the crowd. He stood out above most of the people, so I could easily track his movement. I turned into a side street and made my way back to the camp, where we could dry off by the fire.

It rained steadily, and the lawn in front of the courthouse was muddy from the constant foot traffic. The tent city was quiet, though everyday sounds persisted. Those who hadn't attended the parade sat silently tucked in their winter coats and under blankets, hidden beneath the tarps. The rain rustled through the treetops, and large drops fell onto the tents.

I didn't stay long by the fire before heading to my tent. I didn't see Rinc and Amy. Amy was likely asleep, and Rinc was probably out on the streets looking for something useful. Our large tarp, which covered the three tents, was dangerously full of water. I pushed up from underneath to release the pool, and it fell in a splattering rush over the edge. Mud splashed up, making my legs even dirtier than they already were.

I crawled into my tent and used an old towel to dry Boy, who then joined me inside. I put on drier clothes as best as I could in the narrow space, but everything was still damp, and I started to shiver. I crawled into my sleeping bag and added extra blankets. Boy snuggled close against me, likely feeling cold as well. Everything felt damp, and it took a long time for the shivering to stop.

I closed my eyes and replayed the parade in my mind. I regretted watching it. What cheap entertainment; what a waste of time and energy. The decorations had been poorly done. It seemed like the lights were just thrown haphazardly onto the trucks, sticking on randomly. Were the people who decorated the trucks any different from those in the tent city? Both groups seemed to be doing the bare minimum, lacking the motivation to make something special out of their trucks or their lives.

Still, both groups criticized each other. One side said the other needed to do better and go to work, while their parade showed their own laziness. The other side thought the wealthy should not act so high and mighty and be so greedy. Yet, they stole from others and were, in their own way, just as greedy. I couldn't figure it out and didn't know who was right.

I fell into a restless sleep and woke up the next morning feeling discontented. Before heading to work, I said goodbye to Amy through a gap in her tent. With the days growing darker and wetter, she had been mostly staying inside her tent, waiting for spring. I wanted to make sure she was alright before I left.

34. Everyone knows better

I spent almost all my free time in the library. It became increasingly difficult for me to return to the wet, cold, muddy, and above all, dead-end life of the tent city. The discussions around the campfires were often intense. Negotiations with the city still hadn't yielded the desired results, and through the Internet, newspapers, and street signs the neighbours made it clear that they didn't want us in their area. Our tent city had not only attracted homeless people from all over the island but also criminals. Residents reported stolen items, and despite the city placing mobile toilets by the courthouse lawn, neighbours found human feces on the streets.

I felt myself caught between two fires. I understood the plight of those who had become homeless through misfortune, but I also understood the neighbours who had the misfortune of dealing with us. The city councilors were at their wits' end, feverishly searching for a solution to the homeless problem.

The meals at the shelter were a breath of fresh air. More and more, I kept my distance from the homeless people and interacted mostly with the volunteers. On evenings when the library was closed, I helped with the dishes after the meals, and it was greatly appreciated.

Ann frequently asked me if I didn't want a permanent home. "I want that, for sure," I told her, "but I want to take care of myself. I don't want to end up in a temporary shelter with those people," I pointed across the full dining room, "despite how nice they are, in my new life, I want to surround myself with people different from drug users and slobs."

The moment I said it, I felt guilty. Among the homeless people, I had met many who were intelligent and well-educated. Around the campfires, I had heard their stories and knew that many had simply had too much bad luck or made wrong decisions.

"I don't want to abandon the homeless people, and I want to keep helping at the shelter," I said.

"I understand," Ann nodded.

I enjoyed helping at the shelter. Not only was every homeless person welcome and safe there, but it was also a place where love prevailed. The volunteers genuinely cared for us and didn't judge us. When they made a judgmental comment, it was to help us improve, not to tear us down. They gave their honest opinions so we could change our situation.

In the meantime, I searched the Internet for affordable housing. With so many students in a university city, it wasn't easy to find a cheap room. I wasn't even sure if I could keep my job. My manager was unpredictable, and for every mistake my co-workers and I made, he threatened to fire us. I needed another job. In December, in a tourist city like Victoria, I could probably find a job easily, but soon the quiet months of January and February would be upon us. No, changing jobs in December wasn't a good idea. I would likely be unemployed by the first of January.

The tensions in and around the tent city heightened. The neighbours lamented about the disturbances caused by the homeless people. One afternoon, as I came home from work and walked in the direction of the tent city, I saw rows of people with signs and banners standing on both sides of our street. I slowed down and considered turning around to come back at a later time.

The protesters lined the sidewalks, displaying their slogans to the passing cars. I walked along behind the signs. Nobody paid attention to me. I could read the signs on the opposite side of the road. One of the banners screamed: *'We want our neighbourhood back!'* Another sign, held by two little children, complained: *'My future is in danger'*. Their overweight mother stood behind them. I understood that for her, the future of these children was important, but what did she think about the future of the children living in the camp? Did she even consider the mothers who didn't know where the next meal for their children would come from?

I walked further, feeling a biting sensation in my core. Was it jealousy? Anger? Or fear for my own uncertain future?

In the tent city, the atmosphere was restless. The criticism of our situation, which we didn't know how to improve, made us insecure. I didn't want to stay in the camp. I put Boy's leash on and we sneaked away, unnoticed by the protesters. For the rest of that afternoon, we wandered through Beacon Hill Park and along the ocean.

When it became dark, we went back to the tent city. The street was deserted. The protesters had returned to their warm houses and were probably having dinner. The thought of food made my stomach rumble.

"Are you coming with me, Amy, to the shelter?" I asked when I reached our tents.

She stood up. I offered her an arm, and together we made our way to the shelter.

"Have you ever thought about living in a house?" I asked Amy.

"Yes, for sure," she sighed, "but I don't know how to arrange that. I'm so tired, and I don't have money for rent."

Step by step, we walked in silence. Amy stopped often, panting for breath. Her health was declining. It was high time she got a room to live in. I didn't dare promise her anything, but I intended to do my very best to find housing.

After dinner, I helped with the dishes while Amy chatted with the other guests. Later on, Rinc brought Amy back to the camp and I went to the library.
I searched the Internet for forums discussing the camp and was astonished by the hatred directed at the people who wanted to protect us. On the forums, not only neighbours but also people from other provinces who had never seen our tent city participated.
'They are losers, parasites, criminals, druggies and lunatics', they wrote.
The stingy opponents of the camp were bothered by the financial burden and refused to believe that any citizen could end up at the bottom of society. Some comments were blatantly childish, like silly games elementary school children play. The people caring for the homeless were accused of not having both feet on the ground.
'You're naive and cut from the same cloth. Where does this sympathy come from? There's surely something wrong with you, too', wrote a neighbour.
'Homeless people have chosen this way of life', wrote someone else. 'Nobody was already crazy at the age of ten, so all this craziness had to come from drug use.'
The reaction to this comment made it clear that there were also people with common sense on the forum, people who understood the situation. One commenter wrote rightly, 'The use of drugs always starts somewhere. The real causes of addiction lie in trauma, social isolation, and self-medication for mental illnesses because mental healthcare is either unavailable or inaccessible. It starts in early childhood, often as a result of abuse or abandonment.'

The mayor was accused of collaborating with the wealthy, who were paying her salary, and the police were not spared either. 'The police officers find it easy to have all the druggies and thieves in one spot. That makes it easier for them to make arrests, wrote one person. Another commenter had a different view, 'Only a high concentration of wretches makes the authorities take action. They prefer it when they're scattered across town. Then they don't stand out as much.'

Neighbours accused the homeless people of stealing from their backyards, committing violence, assaults, intimidation, burglary, and peeking through windows. They were probably right. Our group no longer consisted solely of Victoria's homeless; we now had criminals living among us as well.

The provincial government was also not considered innocent. 'The province knows the homeless people are camping here but only cares about keeping the court building safe. They don't care about the quality of life of the neighbours.'

Maybe our close neighbours weren't happy with us, but elsewhere in the city were people who donated wood for our fires, homemade cookies, and clothing.

The camp itself was a mess. The tents were placed haphazardly, garbage was piling up, and drug use was rampant and unrestrained. To better organize life in the tent city, Natasha drew up camp rules. She had found new volunteers and formed an advisory group. Indeed, rules were needed. Camp residents accused each other of theft. There were stabbings, and sometimes, the police and ambulance had to come.

"We have to take care of each other. We need a camp committee," Natasha said at a meeting held around the campfire. Until official management could be established, the advisory group functioned as the de facto management.

Everything discussed by the camp committee and brought out into the open had to be posted on the website. I spent more hours learning about the website, correcting, and preparing everything for publication that the board wanted than I did working on my story. The regular city council meetings, which Natasha wanted me to attend to take minutes, consumed much of my precious time. I was fed up with it.

Despite the turmoil, it was better that we, as homeless people, were together in a tent city. Not only did we not have to break down our tents in the morning and drag our belongings through the city during the day, but we were also able to take better care of each other. Especially for the women and children, living in a group provided better protection against the camp creeps who were bothering us.

We looked like a dysfunctional family. And, did any family exist that never fought?

35. Turmoil in the camp

Finally, I had an evening to myself at the library. I logged into Facebook and saw that none of my friends were online. In other words, Pete was offline. He was still my only Facebook friend. I hadn't talked to Pete since I had been on the news. It seemed that being on reasonable terms with my father hadn't helped.

I missed Pete and thought about sending him another message, but I hesitated. He hadn't answered my previous three messages. I decided to browse YouTube instead and found a video about the tent city. Several camp residents I knew only by face were given the chance to speak.

"We are all individuals, but as a group, we have rights", a First Nations man stated.

A young woman said, "More shelters aren't the solution; we need more psychological support. When you live on the street, you can't show your weakness, but," she added, "there is always hope."

A young couple told the camera they would like to have a house where they could start a family. "Not everybody thinks like us," they said. "The old woman over there," they pointed to a woman a little further away, who was wandering around her tent, "wants to live in a tent and only needs a piece of land to set up her tent."

I let the video sink in and understood that the city council faced a challenging task. There were so many people with so many different needs. They didn't all fit into the same box.

I watched another video where a journalist was talking about being sprayed in the face with bear spray. I had heard about it, but I was at work in the restaurant at the time. The paramedics had to treat him. I didn't have any experience with pain in my eyes caused by bear spray, but I imagined that if it could keep a bear at a distance, then it could certainly fend off a journalist.

One morning, close to Christmas, I woke up to a lot of disturbance in the camp. A camp resident had been found dead in his tent. He had died from an overdose. There was a coming and going of emergency professionals. First came the paramedics and the police, followed by people from victim services who came to talk with us. In the following days, it seemed like we became more aware of each other and more caring. I also found an encouraging news article reporting that the health of homeless people had greatly improved since the tent city was established.

I was home the evening a few men tried to settle an escalating fight. The night had started peacefully. Amy and I were sitting by the campfire in front of our tents, wrapped in blankets. We said little and stared into the flames, letting the warmth wash over us as we dozed off. Rinc was at the large fire in the centre of the camp, where someone in his group was playing Christmas songs on a guitar. The sounds drifted over to us, blending with the murmurs of people plodding along the narrow paths and roaming around the tents.

Suddenly, the calm was shattered by shouting from the big fire. I looked up to see a few men standing and arguing. One of them, holding a beer can and swaying unsteadily, was being confronted by another man, who looked intimidating with his bald head and tattoo of a bloody wound on his cheek. More men stood up and tried to calm the situation, but Tattoo didn't like that. Enraged, he waved his arms and screamed at them. I was terrified when I noticed he was holding a knife. I hoped the situation would de-escalate without any serious harm to anyone.

Some people walked away from the fire, and the drunken man stumbled out of the circle. Despite the efforts of two men trying to reason with Tattoo, the confrontation continued to escalate. Tattoo suddenly lunged at one of the peacemakers, stabbing him with the knife. The victim's scream pierced the air. Another man tackled the attacker, wrapping an arm around his neck, but Tattoo retaliated by stabbing him in the leg, causing another blood-curdling scream.

I watched in horror, clutching my blanket around me as if it could shield me from the violence. I heard a police siren approaching; someone must have called for help. I prayed they would arrive in time to prevent any fatalities. The police officers rushed past our tents, quickly restraining Tattoo and snapping handcuffs around his wrists. The paramedics followed closely, kneeling beside the victims and tending to their wounds. One police officer roughly pushed Tattoo toward a police car, locked him inside, and drove off to the station. After that, the paramedics carefully transported the wounded, making sure not to cause additional pain. The ambulances soon departed as well. One police officer remained behind to take witness statements.

I stayed at a distance. I didn't want to get involved.

Amy was shaken by the violence. "Why did they do that?" she asked, her voice trembling.

I didn't have an answer. Indeed, why did people inflict such pain on each other? Was it pure selfishness, an attempt to release their own inner turmoil, or did their suffering somehow seem lessened by causing pain to others? Or had they simply given up, no longer caring who got dragged down with them? I was at a loss.

"I want to leave," Amy said. She shivered, despite it being warm by the fire.

I nodded, trying to offer some comfort. "I'll see if we can find another place to stay," I promised.

"I want to leave now," she repeated, her voice rising with desperation as if I hadn't heard her the first time.

"I do too," I said, placing a reassuring hand on her arm. I was taken aback by how much she was shaking. "Tomorrow, I'll talk to the shelter about finding us another spot."

"I want to leave." Her repeated plea came out softly again. I sat beside her, wrapping my arm around her, and gently rocked her until her shivering subsided. As the fire's flames dwindled, I decided not to add more wood.

"Let's go to sleep," I suggested. Amy hadn't said much recently and was now coughing intermittently. Her cough had deepened in recent days, and she seemed to be in pain, trying to stifle it behind her blanket.

"Come on," I said, "I'll help you to your tent. Tomorrow, we'll talk to the shelter about finding a new place and see if we can get a doctor to check your lungs."

"I don't need a doctor," Amy insisted stubbornly. "This cough came on its own and will go away on its own."

I wasn't so sure, but I helped her into her tent, and Tristan and Isolde followed. I left the zipper slightly open to let in fresh air and sat by the dying fire, waiting for Rinc to return. When Rinc finally came back to the camp, he looked at me with a mix of confusion and resignation. "What a mess tonight," was all he said before shaking his head, shrugging, and retreating into his tent.

I went into my tent as well.

The next afternoon, I approached Ann at the shelter to inquire about options for temporary housing as a step towards something more permanent. Her response was unexpected. The city, seemingly jolted by recent events, had plans to purchase a building where homeless individuals could move in if they chose to.

It felt like a miracle. Amy and I seized the opportunity and signed up immediately. We also convinced Rinc to join us. He was fed up with the cold, the rain, and the chaos of the camp. It was a chance for all of us to escape the harsh conditions we had been enduring.

36. New Year's Eve

On New Year's Eve day, we got the keys to our new rooms and we signed the rental contracts in the office of the housing association. While Amy and Rinc were signing, I walked to the window. Three stories down, cars streamed endlessly through the bustling main street. Tonight, the contractor would finish the renovation. Tomorrow, we would move into our new apartments.

Amy and Rinc each received a key to a one-room apartment next to mine.

"Here," said Amy, handing me her spare key, "now you can say goodbye to me before you go to work in the morning."

I smiled. "I'll do that," I said, "and at the same time, together with Boy, I'll take Tristan and Isolde out for you."

"You really want to do that?" Amy asked softly. "I won't have to get up early?"

I nodded. "You can stay in bed. I'll manage."

Amy sighed with relief. The last couple of months hadn't been good for her. As she coughed with difficulty, the lady behind the counter looked up, alarmed by the deep expectorant coming from Amy's chest.

"I'll give you my key too," I said, "then the dogs can play together if you want."

Amy's eyes lit up, and I hoped that the responsibility for the dogs would coax her out of her room. In the camp, there was no need for this as the dogs roamed freely and went wherever they pleased.

"I don't get anybody's key?" Rinc asked, and I heard a trace of disappointment in his voice; a feeling of being excluded.

"We only have two keys," I apologized.

Amy seemed to sense Rinc's disappointment as well, and she said, "You can knock on my door every day, and we'll have coffee together."

A smile appeared on Rinc's face. "Great, we'll do that," he said, adding, "Do you have a coffee maker?"

At that moment, we all realized none of us had a coffeemaker, but Amy surprised me by saying, "Let's go shopping."

Rinc also looked at her with wide eyes. I saw him thinking, 'Where did the old, depressed Amy go?'

We greeted the lady behind the counter, who smiled as she watched us leave her office. Amy and I followed Rinc, who danced down the stairs and onto the street.

At a thrift store, we found a coffee maker, and in a lighthearted mood, we decided to celebrate with a cup of coffee at Timmy's.

"Since we've got Wi-Fi here," I said, "let's see if we can find some beds and furniture for free on the Internet."

I sent a few emails to people giving away their belongings and asked them if they could deliver it to us after the New Year. Within a couple of hours, I had e-mails back and had made arrangements for the delivery of the furniture. Amy would have a bed and a recliner, and Rinc and I would each have a sofa bed. We made a list of other items we wanted and I promised to check the secondhand website daily.

We spent the last afternoon of the year sitting by the fire in front of our tents.

"Who's coming to celebrate New Year's Eve?" Rinc suddenly called out, standing up.

I rubbed my fingerless mittens together. My back was cold, and leaving the fire didn't appeal to me.

"Where are you going?" I asked.

"First, let's go eat at the shelter. Afterward, we can head downtown or stay here by the big fire to ring in the New Year," Rinc suggested. "Are you coming, Amy?"

Amy sat wrapped in her blanket. She hadn't said much since we returned from shopping. Now and then, she let out a rough cough and breathed heavily. She shook her head.

"No, you go," she said hoarsely, pulling her blanket tighter around her. I stood up and draped my quilt around her shoulders. I felt the cold wind cutting into my arms, through my coat.

"I'll bring something for you to eat," I promised her.

"Thank you," she whispered.

Rinc threw more wood on the fire and put a couple of blocks within Amy's reach. I fed the dogs and instructed them to stay with Amy. Boy looked at me, questioningly, and for a moment I considered taking him with me. I dismissed the thought and walked out of the tent city with Rinc.

After dinner, I hurried back to the camp while Rinc went downtown. Amy was still seated by the fire in the same position. She hadn't bothered to add more wood, and it was dying out. I poked it, and it caught fire again.

"I brought some soup for you," I said, squatting down beside her. She smiled but made no effort to take the bowl.

"Hold it," I encouraged her, "it's still warm."

I tried to pull her blanket away to free her hands, but she clutched it even tighter.

I set the soup on the ground. "Shall I help you into your sleeping bag?"

"No," she whispered, "way too cold."

I agreed with her. Lying on the ground wasn't fun when you were shivering like Amy did. It was best to stay close to the fire.

"Only one more night of sleeping in your tent, and then you can move to your apartment. It will be warm there," I comforted her.

Suddenly, a plan came to mind.

"Let's go to your apartment right now," I suggested. "The construction workers have surely finished the renovation. It's New Year's Eve, and the contractor has long gone home. Come, let's go."

I stood up and tried to help Amy to her feet. I gave up my efforts and said, "Wait here, I'll load your things in your shopping cart first."

I crawled into her tent, rolled up the mats and sheets that served as a mattress, and stuffed them into her cart. Her sleeping bag went on top. I didn't pack the tent. I planned to come back for it later.

"Where are your important documents and your key?" I asked.

"Here," Amy whispered and slowly her hand came with a bag in it from under the blanket.

"Good," I said, "we can go."

I pulled her up onto her feet. It took a while before Amy found her balance and I dared to let her go. She held on to the cart and step by step we walked over the half-frozen muddy path to the exit. In the camp, we'd had the protection of the tents but now we stood outside the camp, the wind blew viciously in our faces. Amy still had her blanket and my quilt around her shoulders which she held onto with one of her hands. With her other hand, she gripped the cold metal of the shopping cart.

"Where are your mittens?" I asked her.

She shrugged. I took off my mittens and helped her to put them on.

Slowly we continued. Every hundred feet Amy had to rest. Her breath made a screeching sound and she shook all over her body.

"My legs hurt so much," she complained but she kept walking. Slower and slower she walked and heavier and heavier went her breathing.

"I've got to sit down for a bit," she sighed and she let herself sink to the ground with her back against the cart.

We can't go on like this, I thought. I need to come up with a way to help Amy. At this rate, she'll never make it to the apartment.

"I'm going to pull you up into the cart," I said and I arranged the sheets on the cart to make room for Amy. The following was the most difficult part. I placed my foot behind one of the wheels to prevent the cart from rolling away. I pulled Amy up by her underarms until she stood again.

"Wrap your arms around my neck," I told her.

She did and I crouched down to slide an arm under her knees so I was able to lift her. She was surprisingly light and apart from a jolt of pain chasing through my back I easily managed to put her on top of the sheets.

It looked weird, Amy in her shopping cart. A man and a woman, who walked by, arm in arm, first looked at us and then at each other. Hastily, they walked further, but from the corner of my eyes, I saw the woman looking back. I couldn't help but turn my head with a jerk to look straight at her. Spooked, she looked forward again.

With difficulty, I was able to start moving the cart. One of the wheels was rotating like a spinning top. It hadn't bothered me much when the cart wasn't so heavy-laden, but now it refused to make turns and held back the whole cart. I jerked the cart along until the wheel turned straight and we continued on our way. Whenever the wheel got stuck because of an unevenness in the sidewalk, I had to kick it. We attracted the attention of a few passersby. Nobody asked us anything, and stubbornly, I pushed the cart further. Amy was lying uncomfortably on top of the sheets and blankets. I stopped to move her a little, but it didn't change the situation much.

I started to sweat. I had to keep going for two more blocks. I focused on my feet and counted the steps I took. Every step would bring us closer to our apartment building. Off the sidewalk into the street was easy. If no car was coming, I could cross in one shot to the other side. There I would turn the cart and pull it up onto the sidewalk again. The wheel frustrated me enormously. I swore and kicked it in the right direction.

"Are you okay?" Amy whispered. "Shall I walk for a bit?"

"No, no," I said hastily, "the wheel is out of alignment. Otherwise, all is good." I was lying, but I couldn't have Amy get off the cart or it would take us even longer to reach the apartment building. Her face was grey. I needed to walk faster.

Christmas lights were still shining in the houses we passed. After tomorrow, the Christmas trees would be taken down and chipped. The world would be grey for the next two months. Would Amy be able to hang on until the trees started to green again? I doubted it.

I sighed with relief when I parked the shopping cart in front of the apartment building door.

"Do you think you can walk in by yourself?" I asked Amy. "They have an elevator, remember?"

Amy didn't say anything. I bent over to look at her. She looked ashen grey. I didn't ask any further. I put the key in the lock and while opening the door with my back, I wrestled the cart inside. The wheels rattled over the metal threshold, and the door closed itself. I pushed the elevator button. The doors opened immediately. The cart clattered into the elevator. It just fit. Amy's feet hung over the edge and touched the elevator wall. I squeezed myself between the cart and the elevator doors, which slowly closed behind me. I pushed the button for the second floor. The elevator car started moving and jolting and then came to a standstill on the second floor. I drove the cart out of the elevator and stopped in front of Amy's apartment door.

"Give me your key and I'll open your door," I said to Amy.

She didn't respond, so I pulled away her blanket. She held on to the bag with both hands, and I carefully loosened her grip. I found the key in a side pocket and opened the door. I drove the cart inside, placing it in the middle of the room. Above the stove in the small kitchen, I turned on a light.

"Come, Amy," I said, "I'll put you on the floor."

She didn't cooperate. I gently dragged her over the edge of the cart and laid her on the floor. In a corner of the room, I spread out the sheets and blankets we had brought with us. I choose a spot close to the heater. Unfortunately, the items I had ordered online wouldn't arrive until the new year, so we had to make do with what we had.

I helped Amy lie down. Her breathing was getting heavier and was making a scraping sound. I covered her with the blankets.

"Shall I phone a doctor for you?" I asked.

"No, no, don't do that," Amy panted.

"Don't you think it's better to go to a hospital?" I asked, worried. "You're so sick."

"I don't want to go to a hospital," Amy suddenly reacted with passion.

"Okay, okay, calm down," I soothed. The last thing I wanted was for her to upset herself.

I sat down against the wall opposite her. The warmth in the room made me drowsy. I started to nod off so I sat up a bit straighter. I needed to stay awake in case Amy needed my help.

I must have dozed off because suddenly I jerked awake. I sat up, rubbed my eyes, and saw that Amy was lying partly off the blankets, her head resting on the floor. I crawled towards her.

"Are you okay?" I asked softly.

Amy didn't answer. Her breath wheezed and came with long pauses in between. I brushed the grey strands of hair from her face and tucked a corner of a blanket under her head. She shifted under the blankets as if stretching herself, and let out a long sigh.

When it stayed quiet after that, I realized that Amy was gone. Tears welled up in my throat and streamed down my cheeks. "Poor Amy," I said softly. At the same time, a burden fell from my shoulders. I felt relieved. Amy didn't have to suffer anymore.

I dug out my phone from my bag and called the emergency number. While I waited for the ambulance, I heard cheering from the pub close by. The new year had started.

After the paramedics took Amy in the ambulance and I had filled out the necessary papers, I walked back to the tent city. I joined the circle around the campfire. There was laughter and chatting. Beer cans were scattered around, and everybody seemed happy. I hated to dampen the mood, but I knew they would be offended if I didn't give them the bad news. Everybody liked Amy. They were used to struggles and would be able to accept the loss.

"Amy just passed away," I said.

The laughter and chatting faded away. All the faces turned to me.

"What happened?" Jaxsen, who was sitting beside me, asked. I told them that she'd had a bad cough for weeks and that tonight it was worse than ever. I explained how I brought her to the apartment because it was warmer there than in her tent. "She passed away shortly after we arrived into her new apartment," I ended.

I fell silent. Here and there, somebody brought up a memory about Amy. Most of the people stared into the fire and said nothing.

"Are you happy with your new apartment?" asked Jaxsen, probably trying to steer my thoughts in another direction.

"For sure, I'm very happy with it," I said, "It's just too bad it came too late for Amy."

Jaxsen nodded and didn't ask any further questions. He understood I wasn't in the mood to talk about another subject, but after ten minutes, he tried again.

"Will you stay on as the secretary of our camp even though you won't be living with us anymore?" he asked.

I smiled. "Yes, for now. My job isn't done yet," I said.

We were silent again as we stared into the flames.

The conversation wasn't flowing smoothly and I was growing cold. I stood up to go to my tent. Jaxsen stood up as well.

"The New Year has started in a sad way for you, but I still want to wish you a Happy New Year," said Jaxsen as he hugged me firmly.

"Thank you," I said, "and I wish you a happy and healthy New Year too, with your family," I added.

I turned to walk to my tent.

Jaxsen stopped me. "Maybe you should take him with you," he said, pointing towards Rinc who was slumped in a camp chair by the fire.

"Are you coming, Rinc?" I asked, shaking his shoulder. Rinc looked at me with glazed eyes; he was clearly high. Obediently, he stood up and without saying anything, he walked the path between the tents.

"Good night," I said to Jaxsen and hastily followed Rinc. I caught up with him and he wrapped his arm around me. Leaning heavily on my shoulder and talking gibberish, he walked beside me back to our tents. He dropped himself by the dying fire and lay down.

I pulled on his sleeve. "Come on, you can't stay there. You'll freeze."

He yanked his arm loose and kept lying by the fire. I let Tristan and Isolde into Amy's tent and crawled into mine with Boy. Rinc would have to figure it out himself.

Less than ten minutes later, I returned to the fire. Rinc was sleeping with half-open eyes. I grabbed him under his arms and dragged him to his tent. Crawling inside, I tried to pull Rinc in too, but his legs were still sticking out. I crawled back over Rinc out of the tent and pushed his legs in before covering him with a blanket. That still seemed too cold for the night, so I went back to Amy's tent.

"Come on, boys," I said to the dogs, "you're going to sleep somewhere else."

Willingly, they followed me, and I closed Rinc's tent door behind them. The dogs would keep him warm. "Sleep well and a Happy New Year," I mumbled sleep-drunk, and walked to my own tent.

"You too, a Happy New Year, girlie," I heard from behind me.

I turned around. Cowboy Hat stood astride the path. He had a beer can in one hand and a cigarette in the other.

"Come here," he commanded, opening his arms wide.

I didn't intend to accept his offer and mumbled, "I'm tired, I'm going to bed."

"Don't be silly. Can't you even give me a New Year's hug?" he insisted.

I shook my head, but he wasn't satisfied. In two steps, he stood beside me and wrapped his arms firmly around me. He smelled of liquor and smoke and had a sour odour emanating from his unwashed clothes. I held my nose and squirmed to break free. He laughed and swayed unstable on his legs. Boy growled, threateningly.

"That guy is of no use to you," he said, pointing at Rinc's tent.

I shrugged.

"Do you want to be my girlfriend?" he slurred.

I shook my head.

"But," he continued, "you've nobody anymore. Rinc is high and Amy is dead."

Tears welled up in my eyes. "Shut up," I snapped.

"Sorry, eh," he said suddenly softening. "I just wanted to help."

"I don't need your help, I can manage myself."

"Okay, okay," he said, raising his hands with the beer can and cigarette. "I'm leaving."

Drunkenly, he sauntered back to the fire.

I disappeared into my tent with Boy. Just before crying myself to sleep, I comforted myself with the thought: tomorrow we would be moving.

37. The old man

The evenings in the library, when I was writing my story, were the best evenings I had. The old man always came to sit at my table to read. He always asked politely if he could sit down, and I always said yes.
"When will your story be finished?" he asked.
"I'm so far that I can start writing the end of my story," I told him.
"How's that?" he asked.
"I've got temporary housing and don't have to live in the tent city anymore."
"You lived in the tent city?" the old man asked, surprised. "Very interesting. I imagine your story isn't finished yet. The tent city still exists. Or did you cut off all your ties with the people over there?"
"No," I said, "I write the text for their website and I volunteer at the shelter."
He nodded. "Very well, but you're right that your story should end at some point. There will always be homeless people. You can't wait to finish your story until that problem is solved, because that will never happen."
Suddenly, tears came to my eyes. The impossibility of the entire homeless situation hit me.
"Do not be discouraged by what I said," apologized the old man. "Although there will always be homeless people, sometimes it's better to be homeless than to live in a house full of discontent."
I nodded and smiled through my tears. "I know all about that."
"Now then," smiled the old man as he laid his wrinkled, stained hand on my arm. "You have to be happy for every

person who, just like you, can write an end to their homeless story. Isn't there a saying like 'one homeless person at a time'?"

Again, I nodded. He was right. I couldn't carry the whole world on my shoulders, but I could try to improve the lives of the people I was going to meet.

I started to doubt if the ending I had in mind was a good one. I had found an easier way to live, but the homeless people in the tent city still didn't have that. Their cold winter wasn't over yet. Although more affordable housing was being created for them, the end wasn't in sight.

I thought about Rinc, who once lived in a house but couldn't adjust to the apartment building rules. When he was living in a tent, he wanted to go back to living in a house. Now that he had an apartment, would he want to go back to the street? I thought about the old woman who didn't want to have a house but just needed a piece of land to set up her tent. I wondered why someone would like to live like a nomad. Well, like a nomad who didn't move.

I decided to write a bit more and established a goal to have a better job and permanent housing as the ending of my story. The thought immediately confused me. Did I consider that materialism was a measurement for success? Wasn't having inner peace a much higher goal? Or was it my insecurity and reluctance to depend on other people that made me think success lay there?

I didn't know how the future would be for the homeless people. It would be a process of years and wouldn't be solved in a second. I knew the goal of the aid organizations was to have placed all homeless people in affordable housing within three years. I didn't want to spend three more years with this story, but I still wanted to describe how things would end up for my camp friends.

I had built a special bond with them. Every week I visited Natasha and heard the latest developments. Still, the difference I felt between them and myself, grew. Maybe it was because the first two months of the new year were so terribly boring and the tent city looked so grey and sad with all those pale blue and light green tarps over the tents. Or maybe it was because I had adjusted so easily to living in an apartment, where it wasn't cold or damp, where my sleeping bag was always dry, and where I didn't have to sleep with my coat on.

I didn't have to worry about Boy anymore either. He had settled down and enjoyed the lazy life he now had. I could choose when to go outside on my days off. When it rained, I stayed inside, and when the sun was shining, Boy and I went for long walks, enjoying the cold but beautiful weather. My mood didn't depend anymore on how it looked outside. Every morning, I went to work clean, without the smell of the campfire in my clothes, and in the afternoon, I was able to shower off the gross, greasy hamburger smell. I was able to wash my own clothes and didn't have to go to the shelter or a laundromat.

Slowly but surely, I became more confident with my life. I bought a vase to brighten up my house. I filled it with flowers and greenery I found along the roads and in the parks during our walking trips. There wasn't much that I could pick, but one day I came home with a bouquet of snowdrops and crocuses. I felt as happy as a child. Spring was coming. For the homeless people in the camp, things would be getting better, too.

Still, it would take until April before the minimum temperature of that month rose above five degrees.

38. City Council meetings

Negotiations for better housing for homeless people continued. I accompanied Natasha to City Council meetings. Natasha always knew how to express herself. I stayed in the background and wrote down important points for the website. In the days following, we sat in the library editing the text and uploading it to the site.

In January, the province attempted to clear the courthouse lawn and evacuate the camp residents to shelters. The homeless people refused to move, insisting on permanent housing rather than shelters. They won the court case because the tent city was deemed a safer option than returning to the streets, parks and porches of the city. One crucial reason that they didn't have to leave, was the city's concern for the vulnerable minors living in the camp.

At the end of February, a group of homeless people from the mainland came to support their fellow homeless residents. Together, they outlined requirements for the housing they wanted. They demanded to be treated as responsible tenants with control over their own homes. They needed affordable houses without overly restrictive rules. They sought permanent, livable housing without the fear of eviction. They opposed police interference when visitors came and rejected the need for visitors to sign in. In short, they wanted to be treated like regular tenants with leases that addressed their individual needs. They emphasized special attention to youth, veterans, and couples, rather than being lumped together with everyone else.

The City Council meeting in April was tumultuous. The neighbourhood group's spokesman delivered a passionate speech. I tried harder than ever to remain invisible, especially during the shaming video he presented and the valid points he raised.

"Everybody is only talking about the tent city residents, and nobody mentions the people on the opposite side of the street," he said.

He cited several burglaries committed by tent city residents, and the video showed sidewalks covered in diarrhea, with drug needles scattered nearby in the grass.

"The tent city is encroaching on the sidewalk, and people are parking their RVs along the street without consequences." he continued. He acknowledged the valid arguments of the homeless people but pressed for quicker action by the city. "The neighbours feel deceived. The camp has attracted not only homeless individuals but also criminals, which has exacerbated the situation. We want permanent housing for those in need. We want better mental health care services. We want those who need help to receive it."

Natasha stood up and asked for the floor. "For many vulnerable people in the camp, the support they receive is the only support they've ever had in their lives. Rumours about assaults on girls and women in the camp are, in my opinion, not based on the truth," she said.

Another woman requested the microphone to advocate for the children in the camp.

"I want the tent city dismantled," she said. "The children are exposed to the dangers of drug and alcohol use."

Natasha immediately stood up. "Young people face even greater risks when left on the streets. Do you think it's safe in the city's back alleys? Youth are safer together in the group where they can support each other."

Murmurs of approval followed.

The neighbourhood spokesperson requested the floor again. "Tent city lady, what do you have to say about the violence against a news photographer not long ago?"

"I don't condone violence," Natasha replied, "but the photographer invaded the privacy of camp residents. Some women in the camp are hiding from family members who have abused them in the past, and they don't want to be seen. Others don't want their relatives to know they're homeless."

I noted down the points each participant raised. I imagined how difficult it must be for the City Council to decide with so many valid arguments from various parties.

At another meeting, there was appreciation for the city's promise to provide more social housing.

"My only question is," said the spokesperson from the Poverty Group, "how can the tent city be dismantled before alternative housing is available? You can't tell homeless people, 'We're putting you on the street now, but we'll have housing ready eventually.' That doesn't seem like a strategic plan to me."

Another issue raised was fire safety. According to the fire department's inspection report, a serious fire was imminent.

Natasha defended the camp against the accusation. "We work hard to keep the camp organized. Finding food every day to survive isn't easy."

Camp residents requested the province to install a metal fence around the encampment to replace the wooden pallet fence they had originally put up for privacy. Remarkably, the province quickly agreed to this request. Later, camp residents learned the fence wasn't primarily for fire safety but to prevent newcomers from settling in the tent city. They took this in stride, calling the fence a barrier between good neighbours. They even requested panels to paint on.

I found it somewhat naive to think the province would do something like that for homeless people. Everything seemed focused on making the homeless problem go away as quickly as possible.

In July, shortly after the fence was erected, a judge ruled that the tent city wasn't safe. The remaining homeless people had to relocate by early August. The apartment building purchased for them would be ready for new tenants by then. By July, over sixty percent of the camp residents had signed up to move. Only the hardcore group, including camp leaders, refused to leave. They wanted to stay until the province found a solution not only for everyone in Victoria but also for all of British Columbia.

"It is about time," said Natasha, "that after so many years, the province is finally prioritizing more social housing."

I felt concerned. The patience of the province and city must have worn thin by now.

39. Newspaper

Here, read this.

The old man slid the newspaper from August 5 across the table towards me. '*Dismantling of the tent city*' read the headline on the page.

I hadn't visited the tent city in two weeks. It no longer felt safe there. The tents were densely packed on the courthouse lawn. With no rain since May, the risk of fire grew daily, and not all the remaining residents were peaceful.

I began reading the article.

'It's Canada's most disorganized and notorious tent city. Slowly, the dangerous tent city is being dismantled. Despite the violence, thefts, and rats that plague the camp, residents are hesitant to move. The province has purchased a former care home which can accommodate a hundred and forty people.'

One girl interviewed expressed anticipation of clean bathrooms. 'The city-provided toilets are filthy, worse than an outhouse. Ninety percent of the people here are pigs.'

I knew she was right and continued reading.

'Advocates for the homeless argue that conditions are not as dire as some portray.'

I doubted that assertion.

The judge overseeing the case was quoted. 'There's insufficient affordable housing. Unfortunately, the tent city's leadership and organization have deteriorated over time. Also, members of Christ Church Cathedral across the street are less willing to assist. They're afraid of some camp residents. The discovery of a nude woman in the church bathrooms hasn't helped the situation.'

'Half the tents were removed last Friday,' the article announced. 'Hazmat-suited personnel cleaned up garbage, and volunteers tidied the site. Only a few vacant tents remained on the damaged lawn.'

'There's one problem with the relocation,' the article continued. 'Only two of the four floors of the care home, where the homeless people are moving to, are finished. The other two floors still need to be renovated. Over three hundred residents have already moved to the home or been offered alternative housing.'

The housing minister was quoted as saying, 'We've provided affordable housing for everyone and achieved a peaceful resolution.'

The mayor also expressed satisfaction. 'It's been a painful situation for many people for a long time, but we've come to a great solution. However, let's be honest. While we've helped many into affordable housing, homelessness hasn't been eradicated. The tent city was just the beginning of the process toward a solution. Many who never lived in the camp, still sleep on porches and were never on the waitlist for housing. But we have achieved a degree of regional collaboration we've never seen before.'

I pushed the newspaper back across the table to the old man. "I think this will be the final part that I add to my story," I said.

The old man nodded. "Do you think you can finish it by tomorrow night?" he asked.

"I think so," I replied, "Why do you ask?"

"I'll tell you tomorrow night. First, finish your story."

That evening, I wrote the final pages. It was after midnight when I finally crawled into bed.

The next day, I couldn't stop thinking about the old man. What did he mean? What would he say tonight? The day couldn't pass quickly enough.

The old man was already seated at the table in the library when I arrived. Usually, I was there first.

"Sit down," he said as I hesitated by my chair. "I've got something to tell you."

I pulled out the chair and sat down.

"I've spent my whole life surrounded by books," he began. "My father owned a bookstore here in the city. I took over from him when he retired. Besides selling books, I began publishing them. I'm retired now and have passed on the bookstore and publishing company to my daughter. I told her about you. She wants to read your manuscript, and if it's good, she'd like to publish it."

I could only stare at him at first. A fog seemed to cloud my mind, making coherent thought difficult. I broke into a cold sweat, and the only thing I managed to say was, "Wow."

"Here's her business card. Go visit her tomorrow. She wants to move quickly with this," he said.

After I visited her and gave her a copy of my manuscript, I realized she was indeed eager. She read my story, marked nearly all of it with corrections in red, and directed me to improve it. "As soon as possible," she had said. I threw myself into the work with determination. Within a couple of weeks, I had made all the necessary improvements.

40. The End

My story was finished! The homeless people were housed, and the tent city was dismantled. The summer was coming to an end. It had been almost a year since I had hitchhiked to Victoria. Now it was time to follow up on a few promises.

In my mind, I went through the list of people I wanted to contact. First, I would call the lady who had given me a ride to the Farmers Market in Westholme. Then, I planned to email the family in South Wellington near Nanaimo, who had allowed me to camp in their yard. I also intended to reach out to Hunter, whom I had met on the train, and to the pastor and his wife who had offered me shelter in Edmonton. Maybe I could even expand my Facebook friends list. Perhaps I could ask some family members to accept my friend request, but I needed to consider that thoroughly.

Boy and I walked into the downtown area. The summer tourist season was winding down. Another week and school would start. The city was gearing up for the Labour Day weekend and expected one last wave of tourists. Event organizers were working tirelessly to make this final holiday weekend spectacular.

As I walked down the main street with Boy, I watched the Asian tourists with sun hats taking pictures of their families posing under the lush hanging floral baskets or in front of the historical buildings. Unconsciously, I turned onto the street that led to the courthouse building. There were people with cameras, too. I followed their lead, took out my phone, and snapped a picture of the place. Nothing remained of the courthouse lawn; it had turned into a sandy, barren expanse, that lay exposed and baking in the hot August sun. The sight saddened me, and I felt a sense of loneliness.

After Amy passed away, Rinc was my neighbour for two more months. He couldn't stand being in his apartment any longer, so in the spring, he returned to the tent city. During its dismantling, he was one of the last residents to leave. He too moved into a room in the former care home.

For how long? I wondered.

With my story complete, my goal was almost achieved, but something was still missing. I knew what it was. I missed the connection with Pete. It had been weeks since I had last seen him on Facebook. Over the past months, I had only received a message from him a few times, but they didn't say much; only that he was busy with work and spent his free time painting. I barely had any idea how he was doing, let alone how the rest of my family and acquaintances in Saskatoon were.

Feeling determined, I made a decision and walked over to the nearest coffee shop and logged into Facebook.

Pete was online.

"Hi Pete," I wrote and waited for his response.

Sure enough, a reply came soon after.

"Hi Nadia," he wrote.

I started typing, but I saw he was typing too, so I waited for his message. I couldn't believe what I saw when I read it.

"Can you go to the art exposition on Douglas Street?"

"Huh? Now? What am I going to do there?" I wrote back.

"There are a few paintings of mine in the show."

I stood perplexed. I had no doubt Pete could create paintings worth showing, but the fact that he had the audacity to invite me to a show he hadn't even mentioned made me angry.

"Okay," I wrote and closed Facebook.

I stirred my coffee furiously. How dare he! Did he think I was at his beck and call? That he could direct me wherever he wanted? For now, I wasn't going to that show. First, I would finish my coffee and then decide what to do next.

I finished my coffee more quickly than usual. I realized I had been caught up in the curiosity of Pete's paintings.

I threw the cup in the garbage and pulled Boy along on his leash. "Come on, Boy, we're going."

It was only a few minutes before I found the art exhibition. Dogs weren't allowed inside, so I tied Boy's leash to a small stone pole and stepped through the wide doors. A bright, airy hall awaited me. Paintings hung on the walls, and I wondered how to start viewing the artwork. I approached one and read the label below to see who the artist was. It wasn't one of Pete's. I moved on to the next painting, which was by the same artist.

Of course, I thought, they must be grouped by painter.

Just as I was looking around for a museum attendant, I heard someone call my name. I turned and saw Pete walking towards me.

"I..., I didn't know you were here," I stammered, taken aback. My face grew warm, and I felt my anger rise again. "Why didn't you tell me you were coming to Victoria?" I snapped.

"I'm sorry, I've only been in the city for an hour. I wanted to surprise you, but you messaged me before I had the chance to. You jumped off Facebook so fast that I couldn't tell you more," he explained hastily.

He looked at me, helplessly. A shy smile appeared on his face. "I've missed you," he said softly.

I couldn't resist his boyish charm and replied softly, "I've missed you too."

In one step, he was beside me wrapping his arms around me. He smelled of paint and a hint of earth.

"Come on," Pete said. "Let me show you my paintings."

Epilogue

With a sigh, I put Nadia's manuscript aside. It had grown dark and quiet outside. I opened the door to the veranda and stepped into the night. The heat of the day had dissipated.

I looked up. The sky was clear, and above me, thousands of stars twinkled. I thought about Brian's struggle with the meaning of life. Amazed, I wondered why a God, who had the power to create such an enormous universe, would care about us, ordinary people, and even hear our unspoken prayers. Filled with gratitude, I whispered, "Thank You, Lord, for taking care of Nadia."

***

Luke 14:23

Then the master told the servant, "Go out into the highways and hedges, and compel them to come in, that my house may be filled."

Manufactured by Amazon.ca
Acheson, AB